FROM THE
JEWISH
PROVINCES

FROM THE
JEWISH
PROVINCES

SELECTED STORIES

FRADL SHTOK

TRANSLATED FROM THE YIDDISH BY
JORDAN D. FINKIN AND ALLISON SCHACHTER

NORTHWESTERN UNIVERSITY PRESS
EVANSTON, ILLINOIS

Northwestern University Press
www.nupress.northwestern.edu

"The Fur Salesman" was first published in Yiddish in the *Forward* on November 19, 1942;
all other stories are selected from Fradl Shtok's 1919 *Gezamelte Ertsehlungen* (Collected
stories).

Printed in the United States of America

10   9   8   7   6   5   4   3   2   1

Library of Congress Cataloging-in-Publication Data

Names: Stock, Fradel, 1890–1990, author. | Finkin, Jordan D., 1976– translator. |
   Schachter, Allison, 1974– translator.
Title: From the Jewish provinces : selected stories / Fradl Shtok ; translated from the
   Yiddish by Jordan D. Finkin and Allison Schachter.
Description: Evanston : Northwestern University Press, 2021. | Translated from
   Yiddish into English.
Identifiers: LCCN 2021031323 | ISBN 9780810144392 (paperback) | ISBN
   9780810144408 (cloth) | ISBN 9780810144415 (ebook)
Subjects: LCSH: Stock, Fradel, 1890–1990—Translations into English. | Women—
   Austria—Fiction. | Women—New York (State)—New York—Fiction. | LCGFT:
   Short stories.
Classification: LCC PJ5129.S78 F7613 2021 | DDC 839.133—dc23
LC record available at https://lccn.loc.gov/2021031323

To Chana Kronfeld

That
is poetry. Touch it so lightly
that you don't leave a fingerprint.

—ABRAHAM SUTZKEVER
(translated by Chana Bloch)

CONTENTS

Acknowledgments   ix

Introduction   xi

Sources   xxvii

Translators' Note   xxxi

European Stories

The First Train   3

The Daredevil   8

In the Village   12

By the Mill   15

A Glass   19

The Veil   23

Hinde Gitel's Daughter-in-Law   27

The Archbishop   31

Friedrich Schiller   38

Another Bride   42

Viburnum   46

Almonds   50

The Pear Tree   54

Shorn Hair   58

Wine   61

White Furs   65

Cholera   69

A Spa   73

American Stories

A Cut 79

The First Patient 82

A Dance 86

A Speech 91

Sisters 95

The Final Story

A Fur Salesman 101

ACKNOWLEDGMENTS

We are grateful to the Yiddish Book Center for the Translation Fellowship that allowed us to workshop several of these stories alongside talented translators and mentors, including Sebastian Schulman, Katherine Silver, and Karen Emmerich. Our deep gratitude goes to Dick Cluster for his many close reads and exceptionally helpful suggestions. We would also like to thank Nancy Reisman, Wendy Zierler, and Ben Tran for their astute comments.

We would like to acknowledge the *Forward*, where the story "A Fur Merchant" first appeared in Yiddish (November 19, 1942), and *Your Impossible Voice*, no. 19 (2019) and *Pakn Treger* (Summer 2020), where our translations of "A Cut" and "The First Patient" were first published, respectively.

INTRODUCTION

Fradl Shtok (1890–1990) lived through a period of disintegrations—political, social, and personal. Born in Skala, Galicia (present-day Skala-Podilska in Ukraine), on the Zbrucz River, which formed part of Austro-Hungary's eastern border with Russia, she was raised on the marches of a crumbling empire. Immigrating to New York in 1907 at the age of seventeen, she participated in the mass transatlantic migration of Jews to America. The constant between the world she left and the world she found was the struggle to survive as an artist while enduring disdain for women's contributions to culture. Throughout her adult life she waged a battle with mental illness, which would ultimately leave her institutionalized and largely forgotten. These disintegrations, with which her writing tries to come to terms, drive her pioneering narrative fiction. With deft modernist precision, she slowly unfolds the indignities, small and large, faced by women at the turn of the century and artfully captures everyday Jewish life in the Austro-Hungarian provinces and the immigrant enclaves of New York City.

In translating Fradl Shtok's work we have brought back to light an exceptional literary voice. We were aware of her largely through the common though false claim that she composed the first sonnets in Yiddish and from the work of the Yiddish feminist scholar and poet Irena Klepfisz, whose poem "Fradel Schtok" dramatizes Shtok's turn to English in the late 1920s. From our conversations about Shtok, we decided to delve into the stories, and over the course of our reading we found ourselves face-to-face with an original voice of Yiddish modernism whose absence from the canon felt increasingly like a glaring omission. How had her stories not been more widely anthologized, and why had they been relegated to footnotes in the record of Yiddish literature? We decided to embrace a collaborative translation project as a way to return Shtok's neglected prose to the prominence it deserves. As we discovered these stories anew through translation, archival traces of her life revealed details at odds with the conventional biography. Yet, like for so many Yiddish women writers of her generation, the archive is thin and the traces quickly disappear.

We know little about the women who participated in the renaissance of Yiddish literature in the late nineteenth and early twentieth centuries.

Given the often meager archives devoted to these writers, scholars such as Norma Fain Pratt, Irena Klepfisz, and Anita Norich have done important work documenting the lives and work of some of these women.[1] Norich recently began cataloging and translating early twentieth-century serialized Yiddish novels by women, reintroducing such fascinating figures as Izabella—the pen name of Beyla Friedberg, Mordechai Spector's ex-wife— who wrote and published Yiddish prose fiction in the 1890s, emigrated to Constantinople, and converted to Baha'i.[2] Despite a recent surge of translation, many Yiddish women writers remain untranslated and thus unknown to American audiences. In contrast, women poets have received greater attention, anthologized in Ezra Korman's 1928 anthology, *Yidishe dikhterins*, and translated into English long before their prose counterparts.[3]

Women's absence from literary histories, anthologies, and translations gives a false impression of women's literary activity in prose. There was an enormous demand for woman-authored stories in the Yiddish press during the first decades of the twentieth century. They were there to sell papers, however, not to make literary history. While women's prose did appear in the pages of Yiddish periodicals, it was less likely to be anthologized or appear in book form. Prose was the sphere for serious social criticism and intellectual authority, and it was thus considered the domain of male writers like Sholem Aleichem and I. L. Perets, or later Dovid Bergelson, Sholem Ash, and the brothers Singer. From the 1950s on, the male American literary establishment sought to create a Yiddish cultural legacy in translation and largely excluded women. For Jewish American critics, Saul Bellow's translation of I. B. Singer's story "Gimpel the Fool," which appeared in the *Partisan Review* in 1953, represented the best face of Yiddish literary culture—self-reflexive, philosophical, quasi-mystical, and altogether masculine. For decades, almost no women writers could penetrate this masculine translation culture. Until very recently, less than a handful of books by women had been translated into English.[4]

It was two Galician women writers in the 1930s, Rokhl Auerbach and Debora Vogel, who would return to Shtok's work and her disappearance as pressing concerns for Yiddish literary history. Together they had worked to found the short-lived Yiddish literary journal *Tsushtayer*, one of the few edited by women. In *Tsushtayer*, Auerbach reviewed the work of international women writers, offering sharp feminist critiques of their reception and the challenges they faced as women. In 1930, just as critics were envisioning Shtok's obituary, Auerbach reviewed Shtok's short-story collection in the pages of the journal. Toward the end of the review she posed the critical question of whether Shtok's withdrawal from Yiddish literary circles was the result of the "condition of Yiddish broadly" or of "the conditions under which women writers work."[5] Auerbach captures the dual position of these writers, as both women and minorities. They were writing in a language that had no state support and in societies that viewed women as maidservants to male writers.

Shtok was born on the eastern edge of the Habsburg Empire in the multiethnic region of Galicia. Located on the border with Russia, Galicia nurtured a Jewish community markedly different from its Russian neighbors, one oriented to Habsburg imperial culture. Galicia was also the home of a distinctive if short-lived movement in Yiddish neo-Romanticism whose interest in the sonnet may well have influenced Shtok's investment in the form. Galicia was the birthplace of an impressive cohort of Jewish literary talent, including S. Y. Agnon, Uri Tsvi Grinberg, Rokhl Korn, Malka Lee, and Moshe Leyb Halpern, to name just a few. Among these numerous well-known Yiddish writers were many prominent Yiddish women writers, including Korn, Shtok, Debora Vogel, and Rokhl Auerbach. While these women's careers emerged after the fall of the empire, their attachment to the ideals that Galicia had come to represent resonates in their work.

Shtok's parents died during her childhood, and according to Yankev Glatshteyn's account, she went to live with relatives and found solace in European high culture—playing violin and reciting Goethe and Schiller.[6] Shtok began her writing career not long after immigrating to New York, publishing her first poetry in 1910, while living with an aunt and uncle on the Lower East Side. We catch glimpses from the historical record of her early years in New York. There in the 1910s and '20s she participated in the city's explosion of Yiddish literary creativity, especially in poetry, as artists experimented with new forms of modernism. The coterie of poets and writers with whom she most closely affiliated were collectively referred to as Di Yunge—the Youngsters. They pursued a refined poetics of art for its own sake, in opposition to the politicized poetry championed by the engagé workers and their newspapers. The poets of Di Yunge have been called impressionists for their deep interest in simple, pared-down language and in producing poems evocative of a "mood." Shtok's poetry would appear in some of their anthologies. But unlike much of Di Yunge's verse, "her poems subvert musicality with violent eroticism."[7] She frequented the same cafés on the Lower East Side, where she was a popular figure, but she was not part of Di Yunge's inner social circles; women were not welcome there.[8]

Shtok began publishing short stories in the Yiddish press in 1916. Her only book-length collection—*Gezamelte Ertsehlungen* (Collected stories)—appeared in 1919. The volume earned several reviews and garnered moderate praise but also a healthy dose of criticism. After a critical review by the poet and editor Aaron Glanz-Leyeles appeared in the newspaper *Der*

Tog, Shtok was rumored to have stormed into the paper's editorial offices, slapped Glanz-Leyeles across the face, and left, severing her literary ties to Yiddish for good. And the story goes that she would die in a sanatorium sometime in the 1930s.[9] Perhaps the encounter did happen as written. Glanz-Leyeles was also the author of a 1915 essay, "Kultur un di froy," in which he imagined that women's writing should serve men's creative needs. Shtok might have singled him out as a man unable to accept women's artistry; the encounter figures the frustrations of many women writers who might have fantasized such a response. However, what we do know for certain is that Shtok did not die young in a sanatorium, even though this tragic story, recast as a tale of female emotional instability, was repeated in some form or another for decades.

Shtok married Samuel (Simcha) Zinn, but by the time she was naturalized in 1923 the couple had divorced. At around that time she moved from the Lower East Side to Washington Heights to become the roommate of a fellow writer and friend from Galicia, Jenny Bedrick, who worked as a stenographer and later at Columbia University Press, and who would later become a source for Glatshteyn's long essay on Shtok. During this period in the 1920s Shtok continued to write poetry and prose as well as at least one play, *Der Amerikaner* (The American), which was acquired by theater impresario Maurice Schwartz's company but—regrettably for Shtok—never performed.[10]

It was also in this period that she published her only English-language novel, *Musicians Only* (Pelican, 1927). The story of a woman stuck in an unhappy marriage with a violinist and who runs off to California with a crass bandleader, the book was not well received. The brief *New York Times* review declared it a "very poor" work, "clumsy in everything." It concludes that while "the writing is remarkably bad . . . everything is written with such agonized sincerity, such irrepressible desire for emotional relief . . . that the book assumes over the reader an unwilling fascination."[11] By the 1930s Shtok had dropped out of the literary scene—though she was very surely not dead. She was, according to census forms, living with her ex-husband, first in Manhattan and later in Brooklyn, where he had opened a photographic studio.[12] That was until at least 1940. In 2002 Joachim Neugroschel unearthed a brief letter written to Abe Cahan, the editor of the *Forverts* (Forward) newspaper, on the stationery of the Morrison Hotel in Los Angeles, dated October 30, 1942, offering Cahan a story in Yiddish for publication. The letter is signed "F. Shtok" with a return address care of the Morrison Hotel under the name Frances Zinn. (We have included that story, "A Fur Salesman," in this volume.) This led one researcher to speculate, based on a death record of a Frances Zinn in Hollywood on December

31, 1952, that she "had moved from New York to California, married a man named Zinn, and Anglicized her name to Frances."[13] More speculation and another presumed death.

Her sojourn in California was short-lived; by 1943, according to Social Security records, she was living in the Bronx and working for her cousin, Louis Stock, in the garment industry.[14] In one of life's sad circular twists, on the ship manifest of the SS *Amerika*, which had borne her from Hamburg to New York some thirty-six years earlier, she listed her occupation as "dressmaker."[15] From that point on the details nearly disappear. All we know for certain is that in 1966 she was institutionalized at the Rockland State Hospital in Orangeburg, New York, for psychiatric treatment, and it was there that she passed away in 1990. A sad and silent end to an insistently original voice.

Fradl Shtok's creative career in Yiddish can be divided into two halves— poetry and prose. In both she displayed remarkable talent, yet for one she garnered near universal critical acclaim and for the other criticism in undue measure. No less true of her "taut, elegant" poems than of her stories is a keen interest in the inner lives—the desires, longings, frustrations, and anxieties—of young women.[16] Shtok deftly plays out the complexity of these emotional navigations in a variety of permutations. It was a talent that was recognized in her own time. As Kathryn Hellerstein observes, Shtok's anomalous status as a poet was singled out for particular attention in two of the most important anthologies of Yiddish poetry at the time (between 1917 and 1928). This testifies to her "recogni[tion] as one of the ground-breaking modernist poets in America."[17]

Perhaps the single most repeated comment on Fradl Shtok's importance in the history of Yiddish poetry is the assertion that she "introduced" the sonnet into Yiddish literature. This is not true.[18] While sonnets were a curious latecomer to Yiddish (the earliest appearing in the very late nineteenth century, unlike in Hebrew, which was the first language after Italian in which sonnets were composed, in the thirteenth century), it is perhaps more interesting to ask why it was so important to perpetuate the myth of Shtok's "first" status. At its source is a mistake attributed first to the brief biographical sketch introducing the selections of Shtok's poetry in the influential anthology of Yiddish poetry edited by Morris Bassin in 1917.[19] Bassin's simple assertion went unquestioned and unconfirmed until it was confuted nearly forty years later by Mendl Naygreshl;[20] despite this fact, the idea stubbornly persists. As Naygreshl wrote, "Fradl Shtok understood how to pour into the sonnet form, as into a slender Grecian vase, the pure wine of genuine poetry."[21] This passage is indicative of the reception of Shtok and other women poets; a Grecian vase after all is a decorative object, a remnant of a disappeared culture, not an object of contemporary Jewish life in New York.

Shtok was a talented and innovative poet, one of the first modernists to embrace classical forms to explore women's interior lives. The Yiddish literary establishment, however, only recognized her talent because it did not transgress the norms for women's writing in the period. She was writing poetry, not prose, and focusing on women's private experiences, in the premier genre of European high culture, the sonnet. For the Yiddish literary elite the sonnet was an effete European form that did not pretend to social relevance. Indeed, Shtok's contributions to four major contemporary anthologies *all* contain sonnets, and some contain *only* sonnets.[22]

Her sonnets displayed a wide emotional range, with complex colorations and shifts in perspective. Many of them deal with romantic relationships in all their painful inadequacy. She is often at her best when she lets the frustrations of love, no matter how petty or profound, boil over into anger. The sonnet that begins "How evil you are, my friend, my awful friend" likens one such relationship to that of Salome and John the Baptist. "Why, then, does the hatred burn so within me? / Yet I'm telling you now, I hate you." There is no subtlety in this biblical rage. Ultimately, as she dances for the devil, we get an inkling of the nature of her ire from the due she demands: "I'll desire of him your lilac tongue." No matter how deft the smooth talker, he is no match for the acid wit of his wronged lover. One can see why Shtok's ingenious recasting of the New Testament story caused such an impression. In turning to the New Testament she transgressed a cultural boundary. Where other Yiddish poets found in Jesus a complex figure of Jewish historical experience, she turns to the Christian Salome and John the Baptist. In this she was in dialogue with other Yiddish women writers, who turned to female Christian icons, including Salome and Mary Madgalene.[23] This poem is included in three contemporary anthologies, is printed in full in Tabachnik's brief essay, and is translated in the Norton anthology *Jewish American Literature*.[24]

In another poem, one with a subtler emotional palette, we glimpse how Shtok experimented with the sonnet form to give voice to interior experience.

Sonnet [5]

The lamp is already lit across the way.
I lie down on the sofa and think:
What good was there for me today?
And what will tomorrow bring?

I will get out of bed in the morning,
Thinking: *Will you come today or not?*
For every footstep I'll be listening,
Looking constantly at the clock.

And if at the appointed time you do not show,
The serpent will promptly awaken within me
And I will curse you with venomous growls,

And judge your nose to be terribly long . . .
Later I will quiet down slowly
And wait once again for you to come.[25]

Unlike the Salome poem with its sustained fury, this sonnet describes emotions more typical of Shtok's work in general, namely longing and self-doubt. A flash of anger punctuates the mounting frustration, a punctured balloon that only leaves the waiting lover deflated, back where she began. The sonnet form offered several attractions for Shtok: a dialogic interplay, freedom within constraint, and the ability to subvert expectations. All of these are themes she would pursue in some form in her stories as well. Indeed, in these stories a modernist's sensibility combined with a satirist's eye for irony make Shtok something of a cross between Virginia Woolf and O. Henry.

Shtok's collection of short stories showcased her wide-ranging narrative talents. Of the nearly forty stories in the collection, we have chosen to publish twenty-three, as well as the story published in the *Forward* in 1942. We avoided sketches and stories that we felt did not realize their full potential as narrative tales. The majority of the stories we chose are set in Europe, and these focus almost exclusively on women. By contrast, her American stories oscillate more evenly among male and female characters, centering on the immigrant experience.

Shtok's stories often engage in thoughtful dialogue with other Yiddish writers. In "The First Train," for example, she takes on the genre of the train story made famous by Sholem Aleichem's brilliant monologues known as the *Railroad Stories* (Di ayznban geshikhtes). Shtok, however, offers a very different glimpse of the changes wrought by the arrival of trains in the Pale of Settlement than Sholem Aleichem's. Instead of focusing on the space of the train car from the perspective of the Jewish merchants who travel in third class, she observes how the train transforms those whom it passes by, particularly young women who remain at home. Whereas the townspeople embrace the mobility the train affords, sending their children to schools in the West or to America, the train does not reach young Nessi, the story's protagonist. The beautiful seventeen-year-old Nessi believed that "the train had been created for her," that "a new life was awaiting her." But the train brought her no such thing. That is, until one day, looking out her window at the face of a departing German Zionist, whom the community had expelled from its midst, she "dashed madly for the train," heading straight to the man with whom she had never exchanged a word, hoping to reach a new world beyond the train station. Her family, one of the few in the village who believed the train to be a threat, stare in disbelief as the beautiful Nessi runs toward the train to realize the romance she can only imagine from the books she reads. However, though they imagine she's running toward the man, it is the train that is the object of her romantic desires.

Like Nessi, Shifra in Shtok's story "The Daredevil" sits at home by her window waiting for a new world, for love and excitement. She is enthralled by the arrival of a troupe of traveling acrobats, who arrive not by train but by cart. When she looks out her window, we are privy to Shifra's inner world of thoughts:

> Sparks flew as he pounded in the posts, swiftly setting up the tent. *What would this be?* Now he was hanging a wire between two poles. *Why had he doffed his cap to her, why? That vagabond.* But the word *vagabond* felt good to her; that's what she had called him: a *vag-a-bond.* She took a quick, furtive look at him, and felt her heart blushing. Now he is walking . . . toward her?

She is drawn to these vagabond artists, who represent the promise of unknown worlds of desire. She exchanges only a brief word in Yiddish with the non-Jewish traveling performers, but the exchange arouses a feverish erotic charge that electrifies her. Her mother fears that she's been overcome by illness or, worse, the Evil Eye. This is her little secret: "Her mother didn't know that it was him, his laughter, that had penetrated her every limb, like a fire burning inside. She was trembling." The next day when she watches him perform she is entranced by the tights that make it seem as though he's naked, and she fantasies that he's looking directly at her. At the same time, she internalizes a feeling of shame, afraid that everybody there could tell she wanted him. Shifra stands on the cusp of sexual awakening. All the while, her mother infantilizes her with the offer of a childish treat—chocolate custard—denying her sexual coming of age.

In this story and many others Shtok imaginatively plays with *style indirect libre*, or free indirect discourse, the narrative technique through which the narrator describes a character's inner world in third person. Shtok's young female protagonists are overcome with a desire that they fear will be exposed to the society around them. They understand the consequence of breaking with the sexual norms imposed upon them. Shtok employs *style indirecte libre* to amplify these moments of erotic desire and shame, by sharing them with the reader.

In "By the Mill," Rukhl fantasizes about seducing a non-Jewish postal clerk named Burke. She heads off with her friends to bathe by the mill, when she hears Burke call after her in Russian, *"krasna"* (such a beauty). This single word sparks her seduction fantasy, and she retreats to a secluded spot to indulge that fantasy:

> She drew her leg out of the water and studied it. The water dripped off her white foot. She took a sudden look at the blind windows of the mill. *Who knew, perhaps Burke was looking out.* She concealed her leg in the water and dipped herself farther until her crossed braids got wet. *He might go bathing now . . . in his gray dustcoat . . . swimming around, whistling . . . a vagabond . . .*

In her mind he has already entered the water, heading toward her as she washes her naked leg. His single word of compliment lingers as she bathes herself: "She swept the water back and forth. She took pleasure in its heavy smoothness, like the smoothness she imagined clouds must also have. The swelling of the water in her hand, there and then suddenly gone, 'Krasna.'" The word takes on a sexual power of its own in the story.

We see a similar relationship to language and fantasy in "The Archbishop," where young Dvoyre is spoken to briefly by a non-Jewish laborer named Lutsyk. As Dvoyre walks away, she hears Lutsyk's words echoing in her mind: "So many young pine trees broken." His voice haunts Dvoyre: "Everywhere she went Lutsyk's words followed her—over the footpaths, past the sheaves of wheat and rye, far off by the mill—and she was ashamed to get undressed in front of his words." Not only does Shtok separate these words from their speaker as they echo in Dvoyre's thoughts, but they also become a ghostly presence that follows Dvoyre: "They dogged her, burning her shoulders, echoing her footfalls." Dvoyre experiences the disembodied and then recorporealized words as a relentless male pursuer whose gaze she cannot escape. She internalizes these words, and they ignite her erotic desire to transgress Jewish sexual and social norms. These unregulated words operate like the prose fiction itself, igniting illicit desires and blurring the distinctions between Jews and gentiles. These women's desires are compounded by their fear of exposure, an exposure realized in the stories themselves. The narrator delves into their deepest thoughts and shares them with the reader.

Shtok offers a literary challenge to the place of women's interior lives in the work of modern European and Jewish fiction. In her story "Friedrich Schiller," for example, she engages in a rich intertextual dialogue with Gustave Flaubert's *Madame Bovary*, offering a feminist counterpoint to Flaubert's dramatization of Emma's deadly materialism. Rather than ironize and mock her female protagonists' longing for a different life, she harnesses their desires and transforms them into the medium of art.[26]

The story "Hinde Gitel's Daughter-in-Law" makes a convincing case for being a true Gothic tale of Jewish Eastern Europe. Hinde Gitel's eldest son falls for a stunning beauty. The beguiling woman, Lantsi, appears in town and proceeds to upend the old order of things—she refuses to shear her hair, flouting the tradition of married women; she idles in expensive clothes in front of the window for hours on end; she deigns to work in the family business as little as possible; and worryingly she enthralls the entire town, bewitching the men into strange behavior and provoking the women to flights of gossiping fancy.

Typical of Shtok when multiple perspectives are in play, it is difficult to tell what is most threatening about Lantsi. Is it that she flouts convention and puts tradition in danger, imperiling the moral health of the town's men? Or is it that a beautiful, laconic woman can make up her own mind, questioning whether other people's moral judgments are her responsibility? Because of the various ambiguities involved, as well as Lantsi's refusal, Bartleby-like, to utter more than a few words at a time, and the repeated turns of phrase that echo through the story, we are haunted by the eeriness that hovers over the tale.

Her European stories are set in a Hasidic milieu, where husbands regularly visit the courts of their rebbes, such as the Tshortkever and the Vizhnitser. The rebbes were the dynastic leaders of their respective Hasidic sects, and people regularly sought their advice on all kinds of matters, including concerns such as prospective matches for their children, or a variety of other marital issues. In Shtok's story "A Spa," Shtok playfully mocks these visits with sexual innuendo. When the older Vishnitser Rebbe can't help a childless wife, she finds herself pregnant exactly nine months after visiting the younger Tshortkever Rebbe. Even as Shtok humorously portrays the authority of the rebbes over women's lives in this story, in other stories she meditates on how women suffer from the everyday Jewish norms that restrict their freedom and trap them in the home. In "Shorn Hair" a young widowed seamstress dreams of the hair shorn on her wedding day. According to Jewish law, Jewish women must observe rules of modesty including covering their hair in public. In some communities, including the Galician Hasidic milieu that Shtok describes, the norm is for women to shave their hair and wear a wig in public. In her stories, Shtok describes how women suffer the practice or, in the case of the protagonist of "Hinde Gitel's Daughter-in-Law," reject it outright. In "Shorn Hair" the newly widowed seamstress struggles to survive financially as her brothers look on, concerned more with her modesty than her hunger. Despite a lack of education, Sheyndl, it turns out, is an industrious young woman who manages to make a good living as a seamstress. As she establishes her financial independence, she experiments with a return to her natural hair, a symbol of freedom and independence. Day by day, with her seamstress skills, she weaves strands of her own hair into her wig. The slow, painful act of pulling out one's hair to reconstitute it as a wig is a perverse symbol of female rebellion. A neighbor finally notices the natural wig and brazenly humiliates her. Shtok ends her story not on the account of the young woman's bravery and success but on this single searing moment of shame.

Throughout the stories, the threat of freethinking looms over the Hasidic world. The teacher in "A Glass" is starving because the town has discovered he's studying secular subjects and fires him. In "The First Train," the German-speaking Zionist is run out of town, and in "Friedrich Schiller," the father is appalled that his boorish son-in-law is a Zionist. In this religious milieu, Zionism was viewed as a form of heresy, rejected by the religious community for its secular worldview; only the messiah could return the Jewish people to the Land of Israel. Shtok's stories focus on the tensions between the secular world of letters and the traditional world of Jewish belief. She dramatizes how new ideas enter into the border world of the shtetl where she sets her stories and ignite the passions and desires of the men and women who live there.

Shtok's European stories focus on women's dreams and unfulfilled desire at the edges of empire. Her New York stories, by contrast, describe the plight of immigrants, men and women both, struggling to make a life for themselves in a new world. In "The First Patient" Shtok offers a comic tale of a dentist seeing his first patient, while his parents lurk nervously in the waiting room hoping to derive some joy from the occasion. The patient is there to get her tooth pulled, and the parents anxiously listen in on her groaning: "He should have had more practice in the hospital . . . to work with someone for a little while longer. To take such a kid." They creep to the door, peering into the exam room through a keyhole and jumping out of the way in the nick of time as the patient leaves the room. Will she pay or won't she pay? The parents, the dentist, and the patient all perform an awkward dance until payment is rendered. The story captures, in modernist style, the minute rhythms of worry and fear that course through the encounter, defined by the tension between the immigrant parents and their American son.

In "A Dance" the recently married twenty-four-year-old Mayer—now anglicized in the accented speech of friends as "Meks" (Max)—attends the wedding of a good friend without his wife. At the wedding he runs into acquaintances from the Old World, the now wealthy Moyshe and the hard-on-his-luck Oysher, "a man who once threw around thousands as if it were nothing, invested in real estate—and now was defeated." Shtok focuses on Mayer's insecurities and self-doubt as he analyzes the social status of all present and ingratiates himself to everyone. Then his body is taken over by the rhythmic music and he surrenders to the night:

> With his arms akimbo, Mayer tossed his head to the left and set his feet in motion. *Rakhta-rakhta, rakhta-ri-ram.*
>
> A circle of men gathered around. He felt it was him they were gathering around, so he tried to throw his feet out to the side as his heart sang: *rakhta-rakhta, rakhta-ri-ram.* His face blanched, and the rings around his eyes burned with fire, his sides heaving and his heart panting: *rakhta-rakhta, rakhta-ri-ram.*

He loses himself to the rhythm of the music as the *rakhta-rakhta, rakhta-ri-ram* reverberates through his body and releases him from social anxieties. As the music ends and life returns to normal, he finds himself living the same tedious married existence as he had the day before.

Shtok delighted in portraying the anxieties and insecurities of men as they struggled to assert their authority in marriage or grapple with their lives in a new world. In "Another Bride," set in Europe, a no-longer-young prospective groom draws out the matchmaking process endlessly. No woman is good enough for him because his pleasure comes from the fantasy of marriage that unfolds whenever he arrives at the home of a potential match. Wearing his best finery, he is greeted with a warm samovar, a roast chicken, and other delights. In this instance he is the revered match, the desired object, with all the power. The story not only highlights his vanity but also, through its narrative digressions, characterizes marriage as a deadly chase for women.

In two of her New York stories Shtok focuses on her protagonists' disabilities. In "A Cut" May suffers from a limp that painfully disrupts her romantic life. The rotation of men who visit and reject her has left her with a reputation. She imagines how her friend Annie's parents view her: "Different young men are always coming to May's house and then nothing, neither seen nor heard from again. Even that Waldman, the penniless 'writer,' whom people took it upon themselves to feed, even he eventually cast her aside, can you imagine! *Was this an appropriate example for their child?"* In a moment that haunts the story, she slices her hand with a knife. She is overcome by the pain and also fascinated by the image of her own spilled blood. The story offers a complex meditation on how the body shapes women's social world. Elsewhere, in "A Speech," Kuni has a stutter that keeps him silent in the face of his wife and at the club he attends. One evening he overcomes his speech impediment only to return home to his domineering wife, who silences him once again.

In her American stories, Shtok relies on immigrant stereotypes in which Jewish immigrant men are subject to overbearing wives, while Jewish women struggle to find partners to marry. Her characters are older, more bitter, and less charged with erotic desire. Instead they are exhausted by an American capitalist world in which they struggle to gain a foothold and barely get by. Shtok's American stories tend toward more sketch-like portrayals of the shop floor, the wedding hall, and the doctor's office. They explore the new spaces of American Jewish life, and do so with a less feminist lens than she employs for the world of Galician tradition she left behind.

The final story, "A Fur Salesman," is the last one she is known to have written, published some twenty-three years after the rest of the stories in this collection. Set in Canada, it displays the talent of a mature writer imagining a world of fur traders on the border. She captures the brutal ethos of a masculinist capitalism that demeans beauty and warps the desire for maternal love and comfort. It is a brilliant story that shows us a writer who continued to hone her craft, even if she concealed it from the public.

Notes

1. Among these works: Norma Fain Pratt, "Culture and Radical Politics: Yiddish Women Writers," *American Jewish History* 70, no. 1 (1980): 68–90; Irena Klepfisz, "Di Mames, Dos Loshn / The Mothers, The Language: Feminism, Yidishkayt, and the Politics of Memory," *Bridges: A Journal for Feminists and Our Friends* 4, no. 1 (1994): 12–47; Anita Norich, "Translating and Teaching Yiddish Prose by Women," *In geveb*, April 2, 2020, https://ingeveb.org/blog/translating-and-teaching-yiddish-prose-by-women.
2. Norich, "Translating and Teaching Yiddish Prose by Women."
3. Allison Schachter discusses the disparity in reception between women poets and prose writers in *Women Writing Jewish Modernity, 1919–1939* (Evanston, IL: Northwestern University Press, 2022).

4. Several recent translations have made women's prose more widely available for syllabi and should help change this trend. These include Kadia Molodowsky, *A Jewish Refugee in New York*, trans. Anita Norich (Bloomington: Indiana University Press, 2019); Miriam Karpilove, *Diary of a Lonely Girl, Or The Battle against Free Love*, trans. Jessica Kirzane (Syracuse, NY: Syracuse University Press, 2019); Yenta Mash, *On the Landing*, trans. Ellen Cassedy (DeKalb: Northern Illinois University Press, 2018); Blume Lempel, *Oedipus in Brooklyn*, trans. Ellen Cassedy and Yermiyahu Ahron Taub (Simsbury, CT: Mandel Vilar Press, 2016).

5. Rokhl Auerbach, "Fradl Shtok," *Tsushtayer* 2 (1930): 40.

6. Yankev Glatshteyn, "Tsu der biografye fun a dikhterin," *Tog-Morgnzhurnal*, Sunday supplement, September 19, 1965, 14, 6.

7. Jules Chametzky, John Felstiner, Jilene Flanzbaum, and Kathryn Hellerstein, eds., *Jewish American Literature: A Norton Anthology* (New York: W. W. Norton, 2001), 290.

8. Ruth R. Wisse, *A Little Love in Big Manhattan* (Cambridge, MA: Harvard University Press, 1988), 16.

9. A. Tabatshnik, "Fradl Shtok," in *Leksikon fun der nayer yidisher literatur*, ed. Shmuel Niger and Jacob Shatsky, vol. 8 (New York: Alveltlekhn Yidishn Kultur-Kongres), 607.

10. "A pekl nayes fun yidish teater," *Forverts*, August 24, 1923, 3. The copyrighted manuscript resides in the Lawrence Marwick collection in the Library of Congress. Sonia Gollance also mentions this play in "A Dance Reconsidered."

11. *New York Times*, February 6, 1927.

12. The 1930 U.S. Federal Census, Kings County, New York, E.D. 1312, FHL microfilm 2341233, Ancestry.com.

13. Helene Kenvin, "Fradel Shtok: Author and Poet," https://kehilalinks .jewishgen.org/skalapodol/FradelShtok.html.

14. Frances Zinn, application for Social Security number, August 18, 1943, copy in my possession. The document lists her maiden name as Fradi Stock and her parents' names as Simon Stock and Dina Gauberg.

15. "List of Manifest of Alien Passengers for the U.S. Immigration Officer at Port of Arrival. S.S. Amerika sailing from Hamburg, 6 Jun. 1907, arriving at Port of New York, Jun. 17, 1907," Department of Commerce and Labor, Immigration Service, Form 1500A, available at ancestry.com.

16. Chametzky et al., *Jewish American Literature*, 290.

17. Kathryn Hellerstein, *A Question of Tradition: Women Poets in Yiddish, 1586–1987* (Stanford, CA: Stanford University Press, 2014), 290.

18. A. Tabachnik, *Dikhter un dikhtung* (New York: s.l., 1965), 506; Jordan Finkin, "What Does It Mean to Write a Modern Jewish Sonnet? Some

Challenges of Yiddish and Hebrew," *Journal of Jewish Identities* 7, no. 1 (2014): 93.

19. Morris Bassin, ed., *Antologye: Finf hundert yohr Idishe poezye* (New York: Farlag dos Yidishe Bukh, 1917), 2:299.

20. Mendl Naygreshl, "Di moderne Yidishe literatur in Galitsye," in *Fun noentn over: Monografyes un memuarn* (New York: CYCO, 1955), 306; Tabachnik, *Dikhter* (Tabachnik's essay first appeared in 1959).

21. Naygreshl, "Di moderne Yidishe literatur in Galitsye," 306.

22. *Di naye heym: Ershtes zamelbukh* (New York: Literarisher Farlag, 1914), [independently paginated] 3–7; Bassin, *Antologye*, 299–303; Zishe Landau, ed. *Antologye: Di Idishe dikhtung in Amerika biz yohr 1916* (New York: Farlag Idish, 1919), 172; Ezra Korman, ed., *Yidishe dikhetrins* (Chicago: L. M. Stein, 1928), 93–101.

23. See Barbara Mann, "Of Madonnas and Magdalenas: Reading Mary in Modernist Hebrew and Yiddish Women's Poetry," in *Leḳeṭ: Yiddish Studies Today*, vol. 1, ed. Marion Aptroot, Efrat Gal-Ed, Roland Gruschka, and Simon Neuberg (Dusseldorf: Düsseldorf University Press, 2012), 50–68; Zohar Weiman Kelman, *Queer Expectations: A Genealogy of Jewish Women's Poetry* (Albany: State University of New York Press, 2018), 41–64.

24. *Di naye heym*, [7]; Bassin, *Antologye*, 200; Korman, *Yidishe dikhetrins*, 98; Tabachnik, *Dikhter*, 507; Chametzky et al., *Jewish American Literature*, 294.

25. *Di naye heym*, [5].

26. See Schachter, *Women Writing Jewish Modernity*.

SOURCES

Texts by Fradl Shtok

"A soykher fun fel." *Forverts*, November 19, 1942.

Gezamelte ertsehlungen. New York: Nay-Tsayt, 1919.

Musicians Only. New York: Pelican, 1927.

Translations

"The Archbishop" (*Der erts-bishof*). Translated by Joachim Neugroschel. In *No Star Too Beautiful: Yiddish Stories from 1382 to the Present* (New York: W. W. Norton, 2002).

"At the Mill" (*Bay der mil*). Translated by Irena Klepfisz. In *Beautiful as the Moon, Radiant as the Stars: Jewish Women in Yiddish Stories, an Anthology*, edited by Sandra Bark (New York: Warner Books, 2003).

"A Cut" (*A shnit*). Translated by Jordan Finkin and Allison Schachter. *Your Impossible Voice*, no. 19 (2019).

"The First Patient" (*Der ershter patsyent*). Translated by Jordan Finkin and Allison Schachter. *Pakn Treger* (Summer 2020).

"Sonnet"; "A Winter Echo"; "Dusks." Translated by Kathryn Hellerstein. In *Jewish American Literature: A Norton Anthology*, edited by Jules Chametzky, John Felstiner, Jilene Flanzbaum, and Kathryn Hellerstein (New York: W. W. Norton, 2001).

"The Shorn Head" (*Opgeshnitene hor*). Translated by Irena Klepfisz. In *The Tribe of Dina: A Jewish Women's Anthology*, edited by Melanie Kaye/Kantrowitz and Irena Klepfisz (Montpelier, VT: Sinister Wisdom Books, 1986; Boston: Beacon Press, 1989); *Jewish American Literature: A Norton Anthology*, edited by Jules Chametzky, John Felstiner, Jilene Flanzbaum, and Kathryn Hellerstein (New York: W. W. Norton, 2001).

"The Veil" (*Der shlayer*). Translated by Brina Menachovsky Rose. In *Found Treasures: Stories by Yiddish Women Writers*, edited by Frieda Forman, Ethel Raicus, Sarah Silberstein Swartz, and Margie Wolfe (Toronto: Second Story Press, 1994).

"Winter Berries" (*Kolines*). Translated by Irena Klepfisz. In *Beautiful as the Moon, Radiant as the Stars: Jewish Women in Yiddish Stories, an Anthology*, edited by Sandra Bark (New York: Warner Books, 2003).

Works Cited

Auerbakh, Rokh. "Fradl Shtok." *Tsushtayer* 2 (1930).

Bassin, Morris, ed. *Antologye: Finf hundert yohr Idishe poezye*. New York: Farlag dos Yidishe bukh, 1917.

Chametzky, Jules, John Felstiner, Jilene Flanzbaum, and Kathryn Hellerstein, eds. *Jewish American Literature: A Norton Anthology*. New York: W. W. Norton, 2001.

Di naye heym: Ershtes zamelbukh. New York: Literarisher farlag, 1914.

Finkin, Jordan. "What Does It Mean to Write a Modern Jewish Sonnet? Some Challenges of Yiddish and Hebrew." *Journal of Jewish Identities* 7, no. 1 (2014): 79–107.

Glatshteyn, Yankev. "Tsu der biografye fun a dikhterin." *Tog-Morgn-zhurnal*, Sunday supplement, September 19, 1965.

Gollance, Sonia. "A Dance: Fradel Shtok Reconsidered." *In geveb*, December 2017, https://ingeveb.org/articles/a-dance-fradel-shtok-reconsidered.

Hellerstein, Kathryn. *A Question of Tradition: Women Poets in Yiddish, 1586–1987*. Stanford, CA: Stanford University Press, 2014.

Karpilove, Miriam. *Diary of a Lonely Girl, Or The Battle against Free Love*. Translated by Jessica Kirzane. Syracuse, NY: Syracuse University Press, 2019.

Kelman, Zohar Weiman. *Queer Expectations: A Genealogy of Jewish Women's Poetry*. Albany: State University of New York Press, 2018.

Kenvin, Helene. "Fradel Shtok: Author and Poet." Https://kehilalinks.jewishgen.org/skalapodol/FradelShtok.html.

Klepfisz, Irena. "Di Mames, Dos Loshn / The Mothers, the Language: Feminism, Yidishkayt, and the Politics of Memory." *Bridges: A Journal for Feminists and Our Friends* 4, no. 1 (1994): 12–47.

Korman, Ezra, ed. *Yidishe dikhetrins*. Chicago: L. M. Stein, 1928.

Landau, Zishe, ed. *Antologye: Di Idishe dikhtung in Amerika biz yohr 1916*. New York: Farlag Idish, 1919.

Lempel, Blume. *Oedipus in Brooklyn*. Translated by Ellen Cassedy and Yermiyahu Ahron Taub. Simsbury, CT: Mandel Vilar Press, 2016.

Mann, Barbara. "Of Madonnas and Magdalenas: Reading Mary in Modernist Hebrew and Yiddish Women's Poetry." In *Leket: Yiddish Studies Today*, vol. 1, edited by Marion Aptroot, Efrat Gal-Ed, Roland Gruschka, and Simon Neuberg, 50–68. Dusseldorf: Düsseldorf University Press, 2012.

Mash, Yenta. *On the Landing*. Translated by Ellen Cassedy. DeKalb: Northern Illinois University Press, 2018.

Molodowsky, Kadia. *A Jewish Refugee in New York*. Translated by Anita Norich. Bloomington: Indiana University Press, 2019.

Naygreshl, Mendl. *Fun noentn over: Monografyes un memuarn*. New York: CYCO, 1955.

Norich, Anita. "Translating and Teaching Yiddish Prose by Women." *In geveb*, April 2, 2020, https://ingeveb.org/blog/translating-and-teaching-yiddish -prose-by-women.

"A pekl nayes fun yidish teater." *Forverts,* August 24, 1923, 3.

Pratt, Norma Fain. "Culture and Radical Politics: Yiddish Women Writers." *American Jewish History* 70, no. 1 (1980): 68–90.

Schachter, Allison. *Women Writing Jewish Modernity, 1919-1939.* Evanston, IL: Northwestern University Press, December, 2022.

Tabatshnik, A. "Fradl Shtok." In *Leksikon fun der nayer yidisher literatur,* edited by Shmuel Niger and Jacob Shatsky, 8:607. New York: Alveltlekhn Yidishn Kultur-Kongres.

Tabachnik, A. *Dikhter un dikhtung.* New York, 1965.

Wisse, Ruth R. *A Little Love in Big Manhattan.* Cambridge, MA: Harvard University Press, 1988.

Every author's unique and idiosyncratic voice presents challenges for the translator, and Fradl Shtok is no exception. The single trickiest aspect has to do with her modernist *technique maîtresse—style indirect libre* (or free indirect discourse). Take, for example, this passage mentioned in our introduction, from the beginning of the story "The Daredevil." The protagonist, Shifra, had been watching a troupe of performers arrive in town when a handsome member of the troupe acknowledged her. Then:

> She stole away to the square and watched the younger one working, his arms bare, in a flesh-colored shirt. Sparks flew as he pounded in the posts, swiftly setting up the tent. *What would this be?* Now he was hanging a wire between two poles. *Why had he doffed his cap to her, why? That vagabond.* But the word *vagabond* felt good to her; that's what she had called him: a *vag-a-bond*. She took a quick, furtive look at him, and felt her heart blushing.

Shtok could simply have given Shifra's thought directly: "Why did he doff his cap to me, why?" Shtok could also have chosen to mediate that thought through reportage: She wondered why he had doffed his cap to her. Shtok opted, however, for a third approach—*style indirect libre*—in which Shifra's thought appears fluidly in the narrative, unmarked by a shift in person and unmediated by any characterization, but in a way that captures the voice of the character (in this case set off by the second *why*). Shtok blends perspectives to create an intimacy between the character and the narrator that is then shared with the reader. In this way Shtok gives us access to the minds of her characters, especially her female characters, a kind of access that much of Yiddish literature until then had been reticent to pursue or explore to the extent Shtok did. In stories such as "The Archbishop" and "By the Mill" she pushes this technique even farther, breaking down the boundaries between the narrator's voice, the internal thoughts of her characters, and a collective social voice of approbation. In these places this blurring of narrative perspective draws attention to the social discourse that limits women's lives. In this way, her use of the technique is more similar to Jane Austen than Flaubert.

One of the more challenging aspects of her prose is the fluid way it moves between the thoughts of several characters at a time. Her prose passes through reported speech to *style indirect libre* and back again, creating a complicated narrative stratigraphy that sometimes makes it difficult to determine who is saying or thinking what and when. We tried out multiple strategies for communicating her technique's effect. And while some stories did not require more thoroughgoing interventions, others did. In those cases we opted to put the indirect discourse in italics, thereby setting it off from other forms of speech and thought in a minimally obtrusive way. Our goal was to preserve the fluidity of Shtok's prose while guiding the reader through the layers of voices.

We gave much thought to how to translate the Jewish cultural terms Shtok references. The cycle of the year, for example, is marked on a Jewish rather than a secular calendar, just as the week is presided over by the Sabbath; Yiddish knows no word for Saturday other than *Shabes*. Yet unlike English, whose days of the week are neutral words, *Shabes* to a Yiddish reader brings with it a number of cultural and religious associations that an author may or may not be activating in a given situation. Similarly for cultural terms. The word *shtetl*, for instance—the primary setting for many of Shtok's European stories—does not refer to a village, as it is most commonly understood in English. Rather, it refers to the old market towns of Eastern Europe, including towns and smallish cities. These mixed urban spaces of Jews and non-Jews, sometimes with Jews even in the majority, formed the demographic center of gravity of Jewish Eastern Europe. The cultural landscape of Fradl Shtok's stories, notably those set in Europe, is littered with such terms and concepts. In some cases they can be stealthily glossed with little encumbrance on the reader's patience. In others, however, they occupy a more prominent position. We tried to balance the tension between Shtok's European modernist style and the Jewish world that she describes. Where Yiddish words in English now carry with them indexes of a nostalgic and even comic Jewish past in Eastern Europe, we have turned to English equivalents. Where our glossing became more hindrance than help, sacrificing an organic, fluid experience of the text, we opted (with some chagrin) to pass over that story altogether.

In translating these stories, we opted to emphasize Shtok's restrained modernist technique, making her modernist project legible to twenty-first-century, English-reading audiences. We worked hard to bring her stylistic choices to life in English, as we grappled with the difficult ambiguities of her modernist style. More often than not, as we untangled the knot of a story by paying attention to Shtok's narrative ellipses, difficult passages of Yiddish prose would suddenly break free. A cloudy story came into focus as, for example, a sharp and poignant portrait of a childless couple yearning for a family or a young woman's growing erotic desires. Throughout we made stylistic decisions to highlight her artful narrative prose style and chose stories that we felt signaled her greatest talent.

EUROPEAN STORIES

The First Train

Every day new people arrived at the train station.

It had only been two weeks since the first train had arrived at the station. The town was starting to take on a new appearance. They had begun building the railroad two years ago and already it was having an effect. Instead of going visiting on the Sabbath, people would go to the train station. There, you could often hear spirited arguments about the wisdom of the whole enterprise.

The butcher rolled up the sleeves of his kaftan so he could gesture more freely while talking and sketching out on his palm a map of who would travel where. When he realized it was forbidden to travel on the Sabbath, even on the palm of one's hand, he suddenly turned around and headed back into the study house. He told that old relative of his, that good-for-nothing money-lender who stubbornly insisted he didn't want to go see the train because the town didn't need a train, "Alter, as I live and die, enough of this foolishness. Go take a look at the train." Alter answered, "Like as not I'd drop dead."

When the whole town ran to watch the train departing for the first time, it took all of Alter's willpower to stay away—*No way I'll give in to the Evil Inclination*. Later he bragged about it in the study house.

People were still spending the Sabbath watching the trains, but now at the first movement of each train a new sensation took hold of those small-town folk. The rhythmic puffing of the steam—*pfff, pfff*—greatly affected them as they watched the train disappear among the fields. A desire to travel into the world came over them, to drift away with the vanishing smoke.

Many began to leave: some to America, others to Vienna to become respectably bourgeois. Parents started sending their children to the big cities to study. They would come home for vacation as first-form gymnasium students with shabby jackets and white belts. Parents began imitating their children's newly pretentious speech.

Every day new faces appeared, passengers with blond, perfumed whiskers, peddling fresh falsehoods about some newfangled machine or gadget.

Each time Alter heard some new swindle, he would head off to see the butcher and unburden himself: "Some have the looks, but I've got the brains. I always knew nothing good could come of this. The town's gone topsy-turvy, all on account of a train. We were so much better off before we ever heard of that thing."

The town really had been turned upside down. Girls started getting dressed up, dousing their hair with attar of roses and speaking German loudly so everyone could hear. The whole town had been roused as if from a deep sleep. Everyone wanted to travel. That moldy old place, standing year after year like a stagnant swamp, was energized by new sounds. You could hear the echo of a distant world calling. The young men plucked at their beards with a pair of kreuzer coins and started subscribing to German newspapers, which they would read aloud.

Everyone in the butcher's household kept tabs on what was going on in town. In that house there were two factions: the butcher and his eldest son, Leyzer, who supported the train, and Alter and the butcher's mother, Pessi Dreyze, who were hell-bent against it. Nekhe, the butcher's wife, was a hoarse woman who spoke with a stifled voice, so no one knew whose side she was on. But it seemed like she sided with her husband, because whenever Alter spoke she narrowed her eyes.

Then there was Nessi. She was the butcher's younger daughter, a girl of seventeen. She knew she was pretty. It wasn't for nothing that she sat for hours in front of the mirror playing with her chestnut braids, gliding her fingers over the skin of her silky white face. She was delicate. People thought she might break apart. But she didn't break apart. She just swayed like a tree branch. Everyone liked watching her. *The train had been created for her.*

When she first saw a train approaching from far away, she stood amazed and ashamed. A new life was awaiting her out in the world. In the quiet evenings, when the train was due to depart, she would steal off and wait. She was certain that one day some fine gentleman would arrive on the train and take her away—*pfff, pfff* . . .

But no fine young man arrived on the train to take her away, and each time she would head back home with a heavy heart, sadly watching the poplars with their tall crowns bid the train farewell.

At home they noticed something was different about her. She walked around pale, lost in thought, not saying much. Her mother felt her forehead to see if she had a fever, and her father said all she needed was a couple of good slaps and she'd snap out of it. The spark had gone out of her; no one knew why. She was too embarrassed to say anything and swallowed her sorrow in silence.

In winter, when a heavy snow covered the roads, she would run outside, her eyes burning with the cold, drinking in the frost like fire. She would run to breathe in the steam of the train.

Her mother treated her with viburnum to invigorate her heart and made her chocolate custard, thinking to herself, "Let her drink the viburnum and it will do her some good." So she kept buying fresh viburnum and giving it to her daughter to drink. Nessi drank the viburnum and still her heart grew weaker.

The river ice broke up and floated off into the distance, grinding and crashing as it went. The first swallows appeared and built their nests on the straw roofs. A light summery feeling hovered above their nests. Nessi was distraught. The rhythmic throbbing of the train beckoned her constantly, her every limb soaking up its steam: *a-way, a-way*.

Every evening Alter would plant himself by the stove with his friends, eating the butcher's wife's chopped liver and chatting about the train. One time Alter proposed, "Maybe it would be worthwhile, since there's a train here anyway, to make a profit from it. We should definitely get into the export business. If you've got to eat pork, might as well let the fat run down your beard." The butcher shook his head. "Ay, listen to you, some teacher. What does that mean, 'get into the export business'? And what'll you do for capital?"

"Hmph, money. I bet there's a couple hundred chickens I can buy up. Or a couple hundred pounds of butter and cheese."

The butcher gurgled with laughter. "Ha, ha, don't you get it? What a headache. You know what that smells of?"

Alter apparently did understand what it smelled of and quickly caught himself. "You think I'm asking for charity? What, would it kill you to invest?"

The butcher smacked his lips. "Ay, aren't you a genius."

"What's the matter? Haven't you gotten rich off this town? Have you ever even paid your taxes?"

All this talk agitated Nessi. It seemed to her as though they were taking something holy and defiling it. Her train, her happiness.

*

Once a German Jew in a thin fedora, a blue tie, and a Star of David arrived on the train. He called himself a Zionist and talked about Dr. Herzl. People stared at him, mouths gaping, and pointed at him: "A Zionist!" Meantime the younger crowd became fascinated by him—"a Zionist"—and started following him around.

Parents said to one another that this was a bad thing—he was going to lead the young folks astray. They'd already heard that he was going to set up some kind of club. At the butcher's house Alter carried on, "Wherever you go all you hear is '*Mit Zionsgruss*' and '*Hoch Zion*.' People nod their heads and exchange strange greetings. Our own people, who know each other, are acting like strangers. That German, may his name be blotted out, taught 'em that. We ought to break his bones."

He yelled at the butcher, "Well, what've you got to say now? Still think the train's so great? Who's right now?"

When the butcher didn't take the bait and said that it was nevertheless a great thing and that he was impressed by the wisdom inherent in it, Alter burst out, "You know what I'm gonna tell you? Since this is how it is, after all, I'm gonna tell you a secret. D'you know what they're saying in town?"

Alter held off a moment, watching the butcher's fear grow. "In town they're saying that your Leyzer is a Zionist too."

"Who? My Leyzer? Impossible!"

The grandmother chimed in, "How sad it all makes me. What did I tell you."

The butcher bit his tongue and kept quiet.

Later, the warden of the little synagogue caught Leyzer as he was plucking his beard with two kreuzer coins. He pretended not to notice. But when Leyzer returned on the Sabbath to pray, the warden went up and slapped him.

"'*Mit Zionsgruss*,' you brat. Here, take this for your beard."

Off to the sides people were yelling, "That's right, that's right!"

Alter cursed, "Let him and his train go to hell."

The butcher bit his tongue, but Leyzer received his punishment as soon as he got home. Then a few people got together to rough up the German and throw him out of his apartment.

*

Nessi grew quieter, staying out more and more frequently. At home they thought she was out with her girlfriends.

One time she stood watching a train that was about to depart when she caught sight of the German's face looking out the window. She knew secondhand that his name was Ludwig Herz. *Was she just imagining that he was beckoning to her with his head?* She dashed madly for the train, heading straight for him. Ludwig was stunned, frozen in place. Before he knew it, the conductor had shut the doors, the whistle sounded, and the train started moving.

Zeydele the coachman was driving people to the train station when he saw the butcher's daughter riding off with the German. He cried out after the departing train, "Nessi, what are you doing? Come back!" Then he raced off in his horse-drawn cart to spread the news: "Have you heard? Nessi the butcher's daughter just ran off with the German."

"What are you talking about?"

"What does it sound like?"

"No!"

Alter went to see the butcher at home. Everyone turned deathly pale, and Nessi's mother started croaking like a slaughtered goose.

"What? Help! Help! Help!"

Alter grew frightened. "It's nothing, nothing. Quiet, you crazy woman."

"He-elp! What is all this?"

Now everyone started yelling at the same time, faster and faster, *What is all this?*

"Nessi's run off with the German."

The butcher snatched off his yarmulke, then put it right back on again.

"Good heavens, what's going on? On the train?"

"*On the train!*"

The Daredevil

Shifra stood by the window and basked in the May sun. She kept stretching different sides of her face toward the sun, taking pleasure in it.

Shifra was the only one left of five children. Her mother, Sheyne-Ette, fretted over her constantly. Her father was a frequent visitor at the count's and made good money. Matchmakers were already pestering him about a match, *but there was still time. She was still his little girl, singing the Sabbath hymns with him.* He felt she was the jewel in his crown, and thought lovingly, "She is as bright as the midsummer sun, and more importantly, she is quiet and faithful."

Shifra bared her neck to the sun. It had been cold all winter long, and now it was warm, lovely. The sunshine penetrated down to her shoulders and then down, down through the rest of her body to her feet. It made her blood feel like honey coursing throughout her body. She didn't want to move a muscle. She heard a sudden loud squeaking, so she raised her head. Seeing the cart, she let out a happy shout: "A troupe!"

Her mother came out from the kitchen and looked through the window. "A fat lot of good that'll do me! Can I make you a treat, how about a chocolate custard?"

"What? I don't want any."

"Oh, daughter, you're going to be the end of me."

But Shifra's mind was already with the performers. She opened the window and leaned her head out. One of the performers was sitting in the coachman's seat, driving. Another two were looking out from the little window, and two more were following behind, one of them older, the other younger. The young one was well built, with light hair. When he saw Shifra, he doffed his cap. Shifra blushed and turned away.

A moment later, when she moved back to the window, she saw the cart turn onto the square near the church. Afterward she stole away to the square and watched the younger one working, his arms bare, in a flesh-colored shirt. Sparks flew as he pounded in the posts, swiftly setting up the tent. *What would this be?* Now he was hanging a wire between two poles. *Why had he doffed his cap to her, why? That vagabond.* But the word *vagabond* felt good

8

to her; that's what she had called him: a *vag-a-bond*. She took a quick, furtive look at him and felt her heart blushing. *Now he is walking . . . toward her?*

He came right up to her. "*Fräulein*, would you permit me to make your acquaintance?" She didn't answer, but stood with her mouth wide open, staring at him. He spoke first in German, then Yiddish, talking and laughing, laughing and talking. She suddenly noticed his eyes—*no, it was his brows*—how he knit them just so: now charmingly as if about to laugh, and now sadly. *No, it was actually his laughter . . .* He laughed like Lunke from the mill. No, more charmingly than that. *What was he laughing about, what?* Laughing and talking, talking and laughing.

When he bid her farewell, she remained standing in the same spot, unable to understand what was going on inside her. When she returned home, she didn't know what to do with herself. Her mother called her to the table for dinner, to eat a little something, but she couldn't manage a bite. This terrified her mother, who put her to bed and recited charms to ward off the Evil Eye.

She tossed and turned the whole night, tormented by the memory of his laughter. In the morning she woke up ill. Her mother trembled with worry and anxiety. Her father asked with concealed fear, "So, young lady, have you finally met the new rabbi?" Her mother broke in, "Leave her alone. Don't you see the child is not well?"

"Who's not well? What's all this 'not well' business? What ideas are you putting in her head, eh? Out of bed with you." But her mother didn't let up. "She has a fever. Maybe we should call the doctor?" Her mother didn't know that it was him, his laughter, that had penetrated her every limb, like a fire burning inside. She was trembling. "Maybe a chocolate custard? My word, get up and come out to the square. The troupe is performing on a tightrope today—the whole city will be watching. They say it's going to be quite something."

Shifra turned her head so her mother couldn't see her face. That evening she got out of bed and put on her embroidered blouse with the handwoven edges to go to the market square. Her father felt as if a weight had been lifted from his heart. He pinched her cheek, smacked his lips, and teased good-humoredly, "Your color's changed; you look like a little child, my darling, my little treasure." Her mother happily pushed her out the door: "Go on already, go." Shifra blushed. In her blouse she looked like a Ukrainian bride prepared for her wedding.

The whole city was in the market square. Because of the holiday a large number of non-Jews had also gathered. Everyone was watching the wire. The Jews stood gaping: "Such a living. If you can call it that. To risk your life, all for a pittance." "Poor indeed."

Suddenly everyone turned their heads upward: the acrobat, *her acrobat*, had clambered up the pole and started walking the tightrope. He was dressed in a flesh-colored outfit, with a dark-blue silk cape. Shifra's heart stopped momentarily. She stared at him, at his hands and feet, at his tights, which made it so you couldn't tell if he was naked or not. She saw him balancing as he took a flute out from under his cape. He walked. As smoothly and as gracefully as water. He smiled at her.

Could she be imagining it? No, he wasn't looking at her. So high up, higher than the roof, perhaps he would fall, oh! Twice he went across, one way and back again. One time he did it walking backward, and the audience was astounded, clapping and crying out "Bravo!" with all of their might. They threw coins into the cups of the other performers, who were running around in their flesh-colored outfits, every little bone showing through their tights.

The third time, he went across doing knee-bends. When he reached the middle of the wire, he knelt and started playing the flute. "How I long for my homeland, oh!" The crowd stood frozen. The flute played soft and sad. Then Shloymele Lehrer said it was the performer's heart trembling in the flute. It was as if a lost shepherd were passing through the night whistling—if only someone would answer.

When he finished playing, there was an uproar. People got carried away. They threw five- and ten-kreuzer coins into the collection cups. The Christians crossed themselves and slipped their trembling hands into their shirts, untied their purses, and threw more into the cups. The Jewish men and women expressed their exhilaration: "Oh, friends, I must be dying . . ." "I've seen many a performer in my day, at the Lashkowitz fair, in Czernovitz. But I've never seen anything like *this*." Yitzhak had to be forced to remain calm: "You can say what you want, Motke, this is a hell of a stunt. A man risking his life like that." To Avraham Bebik, who had dismissed it with a "bah!" Yitzhak retorted, "Well then, since you're such a mechanical whiz, let's see you climb up there."

Shifra nearly died from ecstasy. She held a ten-kreuzer coin in her hand, one she had brought along to throw into the cup. But when the time came, she couldn't. *It seemed like alms, alms for him.* She stole away quietly, because she imagined that everyone knew that she . . .

Like a stranger she went home and entered the house. Her mother was frightened. "What's happened?" "Nothing. My head hurts terribly. I want to lie down." Her mother covered her with a blanket and sat next to her until she had closed her eyes, then left with a sigh. She lay there the whole night with her eyes open, tormenting herself trying not to think of him, but thinking about him even more. She saw his smile, the flute he played, his kneeling. Finally she saw nothing, tossing and turning until the sun rose.

She got out of bed pale and told her mother she was feeling better so that she wouldn't worry, and braided her hair. Then she forced herself to drink a cup of coffee and went over to the window. Just like the day before, she leaned her head on the window frame and warmed her neck in the sun. Suddenly she heard children cheering outside, then the loud squeaking of a cart. She raised her head and watched as the wagon rode away. One was driving the horse on, two others were looking out from the little window, and *he* was following behind.

When he saw her, he tipped his hat in farewell. Her mother came over, looked out the window, and said, "Those performers are finally leaving. They should have my troubles. What's wrong, daughter? Can I make you a chocolate custard?"

In the Village

Laura Sheynberg walked back and forth between the garden and the house. Just in the past two days the cherry trees had become a riot of blossoms.

Laura, the youngest resident in the courtyard, was beautiful and smart. Everyone's eyes were always on her.

After her father, Menashe, passed away (her mother had been dead for a long time), things began to change in the courtyard. They installed plumbing and an electric doorbell, and on the walls they hung decorative bronze plates, complete with naked angels, just like the gentiles. "Sculpture," they called it. The daughters even began to travel regularly to take the waters at Carlsbad.

Folks said Laura was trying to turn the whole courtyard upside down and inside they were no longer maintaining their Jewish observance. Some predicted that Laura would convert, and the property would be put in jeopardy. Herman, the eldest son, was now managing the property. He started dressing in the "European" style and took a fiancée from Lemberg whom Laura had chosen for him. Laura wanted the property to be sold and for them to move to Lemberg. That's why she only wanted a Lemberg bride.

Her older sister, Regina, a divorcée, ran the household. Because she was kind but not beautiful, she was dependent on Laura. When Laura decided on a whim that she wanted to learn French and asked them to hire a French tutor, Regina agreed, and Herman found the tutor. But Laura had no desire to learn French. When the tutor delved too deeply into grammar instead of looking deeply into her eyes, she took her revenge on him. He might run across her in some corner where she was dressed in a long pelerine and a silk wimple, like a nun. Proud. Barely deigning to look at him. Another time, he might encounter her in the costume of a French peasant girl, laughing and singing. The tutor was between a rock and a hard place; he kept resigning from his position and then letting himself be persuaded to take it back.

Whenever Laura met a new man, he had to fall in love with her. And woe unto him who did not show his affection quickly enough. She would smile at him, flashing her teeth. She would be witty and change her clothes and her whims for as long as it took until he threw himself at her feet.

She would often go around in a dress with a train, wearing gray or brown buckskin shoes that were as smooth as a cat's paw, dragging her feet wearily. It suited her just fine if the devil took him. She was at her most formidable when she looked at him with her weary eyes. The tutor would squirm like a worm on a hook. To use Shakespeare's phrase, she had a "cruel beauty" and enjoyed tormenting her prey. Eventually the tutor had to continue his studies and went away. As a result, the last two months had been dull in the courtyard.

Now, as the cherry trees bent their branches toward the window, Laura finally felt the tutor's absence. She rummaged through the drawers of the dresser for something to put in her hair. She found chains studded with red and green stones, brooches, her grandmother's headbands, earrings made of gold coins, all jumbled together in the drawers.

The gold earrings reminded her of that time in Carlsbad—*Doctor Burg . . . It had been such a long way to Carlsbad in that private train car, just he, Laura, and Regina.* He had shamelessly bent toward Laura and kissed her. *Oh, how he had kissed her.* And Regina saw. But maybe Laura had been dreaming, unsure if he had kissed her.

A peasant woman opened the compartment door and stood there with a chicken to sell.

"Does the lady want to buy a chicken? There's also eggs. Big as goose eggs."

Annoyed, Laura turned her head. "I said no one was to come into our compartment. Go away. I said no one was to come in."

The peasant stuck the chicken under her arm, picked up the basket sitting by the door, and left. All of this agitated Laura. When she returned home, she threw herself on the sofa and buried her head in her hands. She wanted to cry a little. Her father had died, and she was an orphan.

She didn't really feel much like an orphan and was unable to cry. People pitied her. No, she couldn't cry about it. Maybe about the tutor? Maybe the tutor? He had left, said his goodbyes with tears in his eyes. A pair of separated lovers. Tragic. No, she couldn't cry about that either.

But she was still unhappy all the same. Petry, the old coachman, was on his deathbed. And when he held her hand, it reminded her of her beloved grandmother. Even then she couldn't cry. *But for heaven's sake, wasn't she unhappy? When you are forced to live in a village and a tutor arrives, and shortly thereafter he flees and no one visits . . .* She heard the workman clanging the cans of fresh milk. *Oh, the monotony. Every day, cans of milk. Every day, peasant women with chickens to sell. She couldn't even cry about that.*

Now that Herman had married the girl from Lemberg, soon she . . . with . . . with that one from Carlsbad, Doctor Burg. No, someone even more handsome

than Doctor Burg. And Regina? Oh, Regina was running Herman's house-
hold. Herman's wife was mean—she screamed at Regina. One time she ordered
her to leave, driving her out of the house on a dark night. It was raining. And
Regina was soaked to the bone, walking along and crying, the poor thing . . .

Laura burst into tears. Once she had finished crying, she thought about herself: "It's not enough that she's a great beauty, but she also has a good heart." All at once her heart felt lighter, and a joyous restlessness ran riot within her. She went out into the garden, and on the way she looked in all the mirrors, small and large, and in all of them she saw how charming she was, and how nice her train looked with her buckskin shoes.

On the veranda she ran into Regina talking with the maid about lunch. She compared her own tall figure to Regina's. She glanced at Regina's unattractive face, was satisfied, and fixed her hair. Regina, displeased, had no idea what just happened.

Laura left her with the maid and walked languorously into the garden. She knew that her languid gait became her. She walked among the apple trees, touching the hidden buds, which were already giving off their hempen aroma, and stood by the cherry trees. She tugged at the uppermost bough, which was dense with flowers. As she plucked them, a voice spoke within her: "That's forbidden. Every little blossom will become a cherry. It's a sin." Despite her inner voice she kept plucking. Many flowers. And felt with pleasure the young tautness of the buds, squeezing them and wiping the dew from her hair. Their soft fragrance had gotten into her eyes, her mouth, her clothing.

She continued her languid walk deeper into the garden, down the footpath with the pear tree, deeper and deeper, all the way to the edge. There she climbed over the fence and stood on the other side. A rider in a green suit and yellow riding boots was just then passing along the path, brandishing a riding crop. Laura looked at the back of his neck and at the riding crop and willed him to look her way. But the rider didn't turn around. The horse's brown flanks rose into the air, and its noble legs pranced, rhythmic and elegant.

The sound of the hammer clanging in the smithy carried across from the other side of the village. A turkey hen emerged from some hiding place, stuck its head out, and retreated. The path stretched off through the dreary fields.

Laura looked at her buckskin shoes and how nicely the train of her dress suited them. Her weary eyes followed the rider and his horse, but the prancing of its noble legs echoed farther and farther away.

By the Mill

Rukhl took the basket that her mother had brought from Lashkowitz and put her red bathing shirt and a bar of scented soap inside. She then picked up her parasol and said, "Mama, I'm going to go bathing down by the mill."

"Who is going with you? Don't you dare go alone, do you hear? The current is strong by the mill. It's better you go to the Zbrucz."

"I'm going with Chana. The whole town's going there today."

"Don't go too far into the water, do you hear? You'd best hang onto a pole."

Her mother gave her two pieces of buttered bread and two kreuzer to buy cherries, and yelled after her not to stay late.

Chana was already waiting for her. They walked through the market, bought some cherries, which they put in paper bags, and set off cheerfully on the long path to the mill. The path was thickly strewn with summertime dust as fine as flour, which turned their shoes white. All along the path they met people coming and going from the mill.

Rukhl was amazed. "The whole town's going bathing today. Mama wants me to go to the Zbrucz instead, with all the other nobodies. The way the waves strike your shoulders at the mill is so refreshing."

"I don't like the Zbrucz either. The water's stagnant."

They walked through the Christian cemetery, then the head miller's courtyard, farther and farther. Soon they heard the clanging of the mill. When they got to the little bridge over the swishing mill stream, Rukhl felt the slight tightness in her chest of someone about to set off on a journey. The tightness that precedes the unknown.

The water under the bridge churned with foam. Rukhl looked over the railing at the calm green waters of the Zbrucz. As it went under the wheel it became the mill's water. She peered into the dark mill. The milling for the bread went on cheerfully. The smell of rye, barley, and corn wafted in the air.

They walked through the border inspector's booth. Burke, the postal clerk, was sitting in front of the booth in a light dustcoat, watching the Jewish girls going to bathe as he whistled "The Lost Happiness." With barely a glance Rukhl noticed he had very light hair. She had thought it was dark, but it was as light as his dustcoat. When Burke saw Rukhl, he called out after her, "*Krasna*, such a beauty." Rukhl didn't turn around, but she felt proud. Chana stewed.

There were already a lot of people at the water. The shady spot was covered with discarded clothes. On the shore and in the water stood girls in their bathing shirts and women wrapped in sheets, holding their naked children. Rukhl saw her neighbor, Etti, holding her Yosele, who was screaming because the soap had gotten in his eyes. Etti tried to calm him: "What a silly little fool you are. Shhh, shhh, let's get you bathed." But the boy was frightened by the din of the mill. He pulled his naked body free and shrieked, "*Vinye! Vinye!*"

The women near her were surprised. "You're already taking such a little one to bathe?"

"The doctor recommended it. Silly little fool, shhh, shhh, let's get bathed." Asher's wife was delighted by her own child. "Ah, what a pleasure. Mine's bathing happily." She cuddled his naked little body to her, pressing her face against the boy's dripping head with its freshly washed hair, crying, "Ay, ay, ay!"

As the boy's new teeth chattered sweetly and he clapped his little hands against her breasts, crying "*boo, boo*," his mother lifted him up, exulting, "Doesn't it feel good!"

That's how all the little children were taken into the cold water their first time. They would turn their heads away, crying, "*Tay! Tay! Vinye! Vinye!*"— protesting, no, no, no, they didn't want to get wet.

But those who had already gotten used to the water and were wading around would cry in protest when they were taken out. They wanted to go back in because they were cold, their little blue bodies shivering. They stretched their arms and chests back toward the water, their heads still dripping with suds from the fragrant soap.

Rukhl folded her clothes behind a tree, picked up the soap, and went down into the water.

Girls were bathing in pairs and small groups of three or four. Each time they dunked themselves, it was with an "ooooh!" The heavy sound of the water, as if from the depths, mingled with their exclamations. Rukhl pulled her arms close to herself. With each step deeper into the water she felt as if her heart were moving up to her throat. Chana was already bathing and was calling to Rukhl. She wanted to go farther out where it was deeper.

Sanya's wife was floating farther up, near the last pole, leaning against it as brazenly as always, her sheet billowed by the waves. Everyone was afraid to go as far as she had. The strong waves made by the mill wheel crashed against her fat shoulders. When she noticed Rukhl heading deeper into the water beyond the thicket, farther out than she had gone, she called out after her, "Rukhl, don't go so far! I'll tell your mom! I'll tell your mom!"

But Rukhl didn't listen. She went on beyond the thicket where she knew there was a secluded spot with a large rock half-sunk in the water. She sat down on the rock and stretched out with one arm wrapped around the post. The din and deafening clamor of the mill mixed with the squeals of the young girls and naked children. She drew her leg out of the water and studied it. The water dripped off her white foot. She took a sudden look at the blind windows of the mill. *Who knew, perhaps Burke was looking out.* She concealed her leg in the water and dipped herself farther until her crossed braids got wet. *He might go bathing now . . . in his gray dustcoat . . . swimming around, whistling . . . a vagabond . . .*

She swept the water back and forth. She took pleasure in its heavy smoothness, like the smoothness she imagined clouds must also have. The swelling of the water in her hand, there and then suddenly gone, "*Krasna.*"

When she came out, Chana was already waiting for her and ready to leave, because her mother would be worried. The sun had begun to set behind the trees. Nearly all the women had come out of the water. The noise had begun to die down. Some were already eating their buttered bread. Everything was so fresh. The women were all smiling, their bodies smelling of the water, of the mill. Their faces were calm; they felt bighearted toward the whole world. They made peace with the neighbors they had been arguing with just the day before. They tucked into the tasty rye bread with caraway seeds, the sweet cherries, sharing it all with perfect strangers.

They headed off home, some on the path through the Christian cemetery, some through the pale dust. When they met the men coming from the other side, they pulled their kerchiefs down over their foreheads. The men strode, brisk and energetic, arguing good-naturedly about Zionism as they set off home to eat their dinners. The whole town had been bathing. The whole town smelled of the water, of the mill, of the fresh bread and cherries, and they were all friends.

Rukhl walked home with Nekhe and Mendele's wife. As they left, she took one last look at the mill. The night was already glinting out from its blind little windows. Something whistled, something moved among the waves fleeing from the wheel. People said that at night the water turned scalding. But people were too afraid of bathing at night.

Halfway home they stopped and looked back. Nekhe said her strength was returning. The trees in the Christian cemetery murmured, *oooaaahh, oooaaahh.* To Rukhl it seemed that *oooaaahh, oooaaahh* was the sound of strength returning.

Krasna.

Nekhe quietly declared to Mendele's wife that she was going to cook new potatoes and sweet dumplings for dinner. Mendele's wife said she was going to make green peas because they were healthy.

Rukhl felt that Burke was following her in his gray dustcoat. She didn't turn around lest he wasn't there, but she walked restively. She turned her parasol around so the handle faced down and flicked its tassels brazenly.

The returning strength murmured in her fingertips—*oooaaahh, oooaaahh.*

A Glass

The town was in an uproar for some time after the news that Gitman, the Talmud teacher, was a freethinker. Imagine, if they hadn't realized it in time he might have converted the whole town.

People heard it from Berchik. Blessed be the punishing hand of a father who teaches right from wrong. Berchik, who was already married at sixteen and had studied with Reb Gitman, didn't want to divulge where he had gotten the book. But once Leyb Ber gave him a couple of whacks with his belt, he shrieked, "It's the teacher's!"

Really? The teacher's?! Leyb Ber ran straight to the rabbi and raised a ruckus. The next morning they forced him out of the school and threatened to expel him from the town altogether.

Chaim, the youngest student at ten years old, was sitting at his desk studying. When he heard the commotion he grew frightened and fled home like everybody else. Later, when he remembered Dvoyre crying and how the teacher trembled as they yelled at him, he bit his lip. He loved the teacher, who never pinched him.

The fact that the teacher never pinched him made him start biting his lip even more pitiably. He sneaked back and peeked through the window. There would be no studying today. Not tomorrow either. He turned around and went home.

There he found his mother, the poultry seller, at her basket with the chickens. Chaim was an orphan with three little brothers and sisters.

When his mother caught sight of him home in the middle of the day, she grew alarmed. Chaim told her how the men had yelled at the teacher and the students were sent home. She went to see Libe Rokhl to find out if her Shloyme had also been sent home. The next day Chaim went to study with Reb Zelig and was warned not to dare go see the other teacher. For the whole day he couldn't get that warning out of his mind. He wanted to have a look. So he waited a couple of days till things had died down and then started sneaking out during lunch, or even in the evening after school. He would peer through the window. When the teacher saw him and shooed him away, he hid behind the door. That's how it was every day until the big frosts arrived.

Chaim had seen everything. The teacher still coughing. The lamp burning without a glass. The teacher never ate. *Why didn't he eat? He saw Dvoyre eating, but never the teacher. He saw her eat porridge plain. Yuck, you couldn't pay him to eat it like that. He liked it with butter or cream. And why did the teacher's voice break when he talked to Dvoyre? Hmmm.*

One time, after lunch, when it had snowed and the window was frozen, he was peeking through the keyhole and heard, "Papa, it's snowing." The teacher lifted his head out of his book. As he wiped his yellowed beard with his red kerchief, he said, his voice breaking, "Daughter, go to Zalmen Motl's and ask him to send tuition for an eighth of a term. The lamp needs a glass. It's stifling. *Ahem, ah-a-h, hem, h-h-ha.* Here, the shawl."

He removed the shawl from around his neck and handed it to Dvoyre. She said nothing and went off to ask for the money, even though Chaim knew that Zalmen wouldn't give her any. Zalmen was always being asked for what he owed. *Hmmm.* Chaim hid behind the ladder as Dvoyre left.

The lamp burned without a glass. The wind blew the wick this way and that. It was smoky, stifling. Hush. He thought they might have an old lamp in their attic. Who knew? Maybe that one had a glass. Who knew?

Chaim looked back inside and saw the teacher get up and wash his hands. Now he was going to eat. The teacher was going to eat. He had another coughing fit. When the teacher opened the little cupboard, Chaim could see no bread. Not even a bottle. What was he looking for in that empty pot? The wooden spoon held a bit of dried porridge. The teacher said the prayer.

Chaim cautiously opened the door.

"Excuse me?"

The teacher gave a start. He wiped his beard with his handkerchief and said, his voice breaking, "It's all right. It's nothing."

"Teacher."

Chaim choked on his tears and stared at the ground full of shame. The teacher's voice broke even more: "What are you doing here, eh? Go home. Do what your mother tells you."

"They're sending me to study with Reb Zelig."

"Then go to Reb Zelig."

The tears once again stuck in Chaim's throat. He blushed as red as an apple and turned his head toward the door. He took out his lunch—two pieces of bread and jam—and put them on the table.

"I'm not hungry. It'll make me sick."

The teacher got angry at him, "You're such a fool."

"We've got an old lamp in our attic."

"With a glass?"

"With a glass."

Chaim got up very early the next morning and went up to the attic. Even though it was still dark and he was afraid to move, he steeled himself and went up. He searched every dark corner among all the rags and trash. Nothing. What would he tell the teacher? He looked everywhere, when he noticed something over by the dormer. It was an overturned basket. He pushed it aside and saw the lamp. There it was. His heart made one great thump, then started pounding rapidly. He felt the glass to see if it was intact. *No, not broken. What would the teacher say? Who knew what the teacher would say?*

He hid the lamp under his coat and went back down. The snow sparkled in his eyes. He ran off as fast as his legs could carry him. He was gushing with pride to bring the teacher a lamp with a glass, an unbroken glass. He even started singing.

Shloyme Perets, the synagogue sexton, ran into him on the way. "You mustn't sing so early in the morning. If you sing too early, all that's left is to cry. Who are you bringing that lamp to?" Chaim was so cheerful that even Shloyme Perets with his blind eye was charmed. Chaim felt like someone important, someone whom people needed. Here he was bringing the teacher a lamp, with a glass.

"Who are you bringing that lamp to?"

"No one."

"Look how you're holding it. You're going to drop it."

Chaim felt insulted. *He was going to drop a lamp? Was he some little kid?* He was annoyed at the sexton. So he clutched the lamp even tighter—he'd show that sexton that he knew how to hold a lamp. And as he chatted with the sexton about a Chanukah dreidel, his heart felt like a bird ready to soar. Then he cockily brandished the lamp, and something made a crashing sound. Until Chaim remembered what he was holding in his hand, he thought that the crash had come from the distance. *Why did he feel as if some part of his heart had torn away?*

The glass had fallen and shattered. Blind Shloyme Perets gloated, "Oho, I told you you shouldn't hold the lamp like that. *Hee, hee, hee.* Oh, is your mother going to give it to you now. *Hee, hee, hee.* If you sing too early all that's left is to cry."

Chaim stood in that spot for a long time. As he thought about it, he clenched the lamp tightly in his little blue fingers and felt two frozen tears on his cheeks.

If you sing too early, all that's left is to cry. Shloyme Perets should drop dead . . . No, he mustn't curse . . . Hush . . . What would the teacher say? Who knew what the teacher would say?

Hmmm.

Warm tears rolled down his frozen cheeks like little potatoes, one after the other. He kept looking again and again at the shards of glass, and then he left. On the way to the teacher's he felt as if every step were a waste. After all, he wasn't needed anymore. A lamp without a glass. The teacher already had *that*; he didn't need his. Chaim looked for the deepest places in the snow and stuck his feet in. Let him sink down. Let his boots get stuck—then he'd have to walk barefoot. What did he need boots for?

He stomped his boots on the sharp stones he found along the way. Levitsky's dog came out and barked at him. This time he didn't run away as he usually did. *If only the dog would bite him. If only, if only, please God . . . What would the teacher say? Who knew what the teacher would say?*

Near the miller's place, when the geese stretched their necks out at him, he thought, if only they'd swallow me up, please God.

He stood in the entryway next to the ladder and looked down at the blackened wick. *How had he let it fall? How? He had only waved it around. Let those hands wither that waved the glass around. If only they would wither. If only, if only, please God. You're not supposed to wave a glass around. No, no . . . He was going to suffocate. Dear God, make a miracle . . . Just this once . . . I'll never ask again . . .*

The teacher opened the door. Standing next to him, Chaim blushed as red as an apple.

"Teacher, I . . . the lamp."

"Without a glass?"

"Without a glass."

The Veil

The veil and the myrtle were brought to them at home. Manya got a bowl of water and put the myrtle in.

Beyle, Tsirel's daughter, was getting married today. Her family thought it a miracle when she had gotten engaged some four weeks back. Beyle was an older girl. No one had expected her to get married.

"True, he's not a young man, but he's got a shop with quality merchandise," explained Zlate, Manya's mother.

Manya was not really pleased. She knew she wouldn't be going to the wedding even though they were relatives. Ever since their father, Yitskhok, disappeared and Zlate became an *agune*, an abandoned wife, she wouldn't let the children hold their heads up in public. They never went to weddings. They were never allowed to hear the musicians playing except from a distance. Manya loved the music. More than once she would sneak downstairs at night and open the window, listening for the musicians as they roamed the town, gradually getting farther and farther away—as they played some sad piece that drifted in through the window, leaving people unable to sleep for the rest of the night; as they sent hearts into such distress and confusion about what they wanted.

Manya had a sweet face. Her heart was always aflutter. Why did it flutter? Sometimes it was the ringing of the scythes on a summer's eve, or a handsome peasant atop a hay wagon, or a song of grief coming through a window at night. She always wanted to attend a wedding, and always her mother would not let her go. Where *did* she let her go? Well, not to the circus when it came to town. She had to sit at home helping her mother mend other people's laundry.

As a result she never learned how to behave among people. On the Sabbath fete before the wedding she wanted to take a second helping of *flodn* cake, so it was good her mother stepped on her foot to stop her.

Sunday morning Tsirel herself came over and burst into tears, begging Zlate that at the very least she should let Manya come to the wedding. They had no one to be the garland maid. Zlate's face had a strange look as she considered it and then said, "We'll see." When the children heard that "we'll see," they started pleading with her. Their neighbor Pessi and her daughter Leyetsi also started pleading. Tsirel wiped her eyes. But Manya kept quiet. She was the eldest, and she understood very well, though her heart was aflutter and her face had gone pale. Zlate took a look at Manya and said, "Go iron that white dress of yours, garland maid."

So the veil and the myrtle were brought to them. The house was turned topsy-turvy. Leyetsi came over and hugged Manya, telling her that that new flutist would be playing at the wedding. Who was the new flutist? A student studying in Vienna. He had gotten in a row with his father and gone off to some city abroad to become a musician, just to spite his father. Oh, how he played!

Manya leaned over the water bowl and smelled the myrtle. The small green twigs had swollen in the water and filled the house with a fragrance redolent of a bride, a white veil, preserves, and a wedding canopy.

Rosa, the hairdresser, arrived to arrange the garland. She took some gray thread and braided the branches, winding them around Manya's head and connecting them at her forehead to look like a crown. Then she took the white veil out of a box and shook it out. The room filled with the veil and set Manya's heart to fluttering—*so much veil* . . .

She stood there motionless out of respect for its whiteness and delicacy. She then urged the neighbors who had arrived into the corners of the room. She trembled at the way Rosa had shaken the veil out across the entire room.

"Rosa, the veil will get dirty. Spread something out underneath it."

"What should I use?"

"My white dress."

"You're crazy!"

Later, the veil lay spread out with the green garland dripping water onto the veil's white crown.

And Manya's heart fluttered at the veil, that it could cover an entire room, and it was so . . . *ahhhhh* . . .

"*Ahhhhh* . . ."

When it was time for her to bring the veil to the bride, she carried it like a breath of air that might dissolve at any moment, fading into nothingness. And when as a garland maid she put the garland on the bride, she lowered her head so that the water from the myrtle might run off onto her own head.

The musicians were playing at the bride's house. Dressed in white, Manya stood by a lamp that reddened her face. She avoided looking at the new flutist, but she held her head so that she could see whether he was looking at her.

She heard nothing but his flute. Then, she suddenly grew embarrassed in front of the flute—embarrassed at Tsirel, her relative, for the fact that she was constantly going to the Aid Society for interest-free loans for her shop; that she didn't have a tooth in her mouth; that her husband, Leyzer, was caught up in that business with the Carlsbad waters; and that her son, Yosi, went around with a bandage around his neck.

And she was embarrassed that everyone was crying, as if the sun shining on a frosty roof had set everything to melting and trickling down.

It seemed to her as if Leyzer's long face looked as it did on Rosh Hashanah during the *tashlikh* ceremony, when she saw him shaking his sins into the Zbrucz, ridding the yoke from his shoulders and getting square with God.

Then she turned her eyes to the musicians, whose playing had sent more than one Jewish bride off to her grave. She sensed they were smiling behind their mustaches and felt that it was true what people said, that the trumpet sounded, "This will be for you as well, this will be for you as well . . ."; that the flute cried, "Oh, how ill you'll fare!"; and that the bass raged, "Just like that, just like that . . ."

The wedding meal was at the hall. They arrived by horse-drawn carriage. Manya sat next to the bride, constantly adjusting the garland, moving the veil from her shoulders, from over her face, spreading it over her legs, gathering it up around her knees, all the while wiping away the drops of water that fell from the myrtle onto the bride's forehead. She felt a burden as big as the world; she hadn't had any idea of what a garland maid was really supposed to do. It wasn't just looking after the bride's garland; she had to take care of the bride's veil as well.

And once inside, again she heard nothing but his flute. She didn't look at him, but she could feel him watching her. After she had danced Les Lanciers, she curtseyed politely before him.

She kept finding herself going over to the musicians—a garland maid must see to it that everyone dances. Along the way, she stole a glance at him. She saw his chestnut hair, dark eyes, and heavy lower lip. She felt him bowing to her, close, too close . . .

"*Fräulein, Sie tanzt wunderschön*—Miss, you dance beautifully."

He then spoke so many words to her, passionate words, right in her ear. At one point he said, "*Es ist ja lieber Unsinn*—It's all rather ridiculous."

He burst out in a soft rasping laugh, straight from the heart. That passionate laughter right in her ear made her ears flush deeply.

"It's all ra-ther ridiculous . . . ra-ther . . ."

Leyetsi came over and called her away: "I have to tell you a secret." She leaned in closer to her face, "The flutist, he was asking about you. 'Who is that girl? Oh she is a lovely girl.'"

Manya looked at Leyetsi's face with its dark teeth and thought those dark teeth might be charming after all.

She walked over to the bride, put her own hot face behind the veil, and adjusted the myrtle on the bride's head.

All of a sudden her mother came over, wearing her weekday clothes, and told her that it was three o'clock and she should come home. The children had already been carried home asleep.

She stood there in a daze, not knowing what was happening to her. As the music played, it seemed so alien to her, so distant. All at once a gray sheepskin coat appeared, a man's coat, and Manya put her arms into it, letting her mother wrap it around her neck, and it seemed to her that the worst part was her mother wrapping it around her neck.

Hinde Gitel's Daughter-in-Law

The moment Hinde Gitel returned with her new daughter-in-law, the entire town was taken aback: Hinde Gitel's daughter-in-law was a beauty.

Alter's wife trembled when she saw her for the first time. She told the other women that being near that radiant face was like being in the presence of royalty.

Did anyone know her name?

"Lantsi."

"Lantsi?"

Hinde Gitel, a widow, sold dairy products from her home. Every year her eldest son, Chaim, set up a stand at the market to sell their dairy goods.

Apart from Chaim there was also Shloymele, all of sixteen.

Hinde Gitel was frightened by this new daughter-in-law. Chaim had wanted her as soon as he set his eyes on her. Even when they learned the matchmaker had lied and there was no dowry, he wouldn't hear of getting out of it. They got married in that distant city anyway. That's why Hinde Gitel was so frightened. She thought to herself, *What'll happen later . . .*

Soon after the wedding Hinde Gitel hinted that maybe Lantsi should, according to Jewish tradition, finally cut off her hair. But Lantsi stiffened and in a strange voice said, "No." And that's how it stood. She did not cut off her hair. Hinde Gitel was beside herself, embarrassed to go into town. But Lantsi's parents had graciously invited them to pay a visit. Once there, Lantsi's mother had managed to persuade her to take along a wig to wear over her hair.

However, as soon as Lantsi had arrived at her mother-in-law's that next morning, much to Hinde Gitel's dismay, she hid the wig in a drawer, put on a red silk bonnet with cream-colored lace that didn't entirely cover her hair, and seated herself beside the window. Hinde Gitel walked around sighing. When a braid dared to appear from among the lace, she rushed over to Lantsi, chiding her to conceal her hair: "It's not allowed, daughter. A Jewish girl is not permitted to go about with her hair."

But when Lantsi felt her mother-in-law's hand, she wrested her head away and gave her a look of such haughtiness that it left Hinde Gitel utterly deflated. Then Lantsi uttered three distinct words: "Let me be."

From then on, Hinde Gitel left her alone.

Everyone else rushed to get a look at her. Women and men alike made any excuse to stop by her window; they came to buy milk just to see her. As soon as they looked into her face they were unable to tear their eyes away.

The butcher who lived behind Hinde Gitel's house used to enter the slaughterhouse by the back alley. He convinced himself that going through the street was actually faster so every day he'd have to take a look through Hinde Gitel's window. In truth, those looks backfired on him. He suffered in silence, punishing himself with half days of fasting. But still he had to look.

Everyone felt compelled to look. Lantsi drew all to the window so they could look at her and tremble with fear. They suspected some sort of spell. With eyes gleaming and mouths agape they whispered to one another about her.

She never went outside. She simply stood by the window doing nothing. She could spend a whole day by the window washing her hands, water spattering her silk dress. This bothered Hinde Gitel.

"At home, daughter, it's a sin to go about in a silk dress. And your hands are as pure as silver; daughter, you mustn't wash them so much."

Lantsi responded with measured words that she hadn't made these clothes just to be kept in the closet and that she would go on washing her hands. She was wary of damaging her dress, but she continued to lather and wash her hands.

The whole thing was obviously beneath her dignity. *That house with all the dairy goods. It was no concern of hers.* She was constantly preoccupied with herself. Her inner life was a mystery to all but herself. Only she understood why she acted distantly, repulsed at the idea of touching anything, as if all of it was contaminated.

Chaim was an ordinary young man with a small blond beard, who faithfully looked after his business. Until now he had been a young man like any other, but once people caught sight of his young wife, they began looking at him differently. They started paying closer attention, listening to him with greater respect, and never interrupting. They looked for meaning in everything he said and thought, *There really must be something to him after all to have such a wife.*

People started showing off in front of him, displaying their cleverness, one-upping each other, calling out each other's mistakes so that Chaim might see and maybe tell her about them.

Alter's wife recounted one time when she looked in through the window and saw the young wife get up at night, braid her hair, put on that red silk dress, and walk into the priest's garden. There she busied herself with the flowers, collecting the dew and washing her face. She then went from one garden to the next the whole night, engrossed in the flowers and washing her face. *Well, it wasn't for nothing her face glowed like that.*

Some said she bathed in milk, immersing herself every night. *It wasn't for nothing that her hands were as pure as silver.*

"Haven't you seen how she braids her hair at night?"

"Seen it myself."

"It's not for nothing she walks around wearing a bonnet. Under that bonnet are two long braids. Didn't cut them off. Such impiety. A Jewish girl."

Chaim's younger brother, Shloymele, had been the kind of person to burst out laughing at any little thing. As soon as Lantsi had come into their house, he fell apart. He stopped eating regular meals and turned pale. For the most part he avoided the house. It was only when he went off into the gardens by himself that he wasn't embarrassed to lift his head because there was no one there to look him in the eye.

Lantsi saw he was falling apart and knew why. After all, she was used to this. So she began paying more attention to him than anyone else and bossing him around.

Once, when he was sitting in the other room, a girl came in for a quart of milk. Lantsi's great beauty made the girl so self-conscious that she hid her pitcher among the folds of her dress. Shloymele ran in from the other room, took the pitcher from the girl, and measured out a quart of milk.

When the girl handed Lantsi the six kreuzer, Lantsi didn't want to take them and said to Shloymele, "Take it."

"No, it is for you to take."

"You don't need to be so formal with your sister-in-law. Go ahead and take it."

He took the six kreuzer and for the rest of the day went about in a daze— *You don't need to be so formal with your sister-in-law . . . go ahead and take it . . .*

That evening Shloymele paid closer attention to Chaim. He saw a strange look in Chaim's eyes that he had never seen before. His brother had somehow become more dignified. He looked like he wanted to take the world by storm. He kept talking about Lashkowitz, how he was in a hurry to go to Lashkowitz to get gifts for her.

And her? Lantsi? She didn't look at him. She just kept brushing off her dress, and running her fingers through her hair. She wasn't going to wear any wigs.

One time, after supper, when Chaim went out to take care of the cows, she called to him, "Shloymele. One of my shoes has been pinching me. The white satin one. Go and take it to the cobbler, will you?"

She took out a white satin shoe and handed it to him.

"Look, here's where it's pinching me." As she leaned over him, he could smell her hair. His head reeled; he thought he was going to die.

She leaned over him, closer and closer, holding her satin shoe, letting him smell her hair.

Her voice jolted him: "Shloymele!"

It was the first time she had called him by his name.

The sound of her "Shloymele" never left him alone. It wound itself around him like a snake, a sweet snake, squeezing the life out of him.

In the cobbler's dark vestibule he took the shoe out of its box, removed his velvet hat, and put the shoe inside.

His forehead started to burn.

There she sat in her bonnet, looking out the window. Whenever a woman came in for some milk, she would stand up, take a look at the woman and at her milk pails, and say haughtily, "Measure it out yourself!" Once the astonished woman had measured her milk and paid the six kreuzer, Lantsi would put the money in a cup on the sideboard, look the woman in the eyes, wash her hands, and go back to the window.

In town people began to say that it was not for nothing that their neighbor Menachem had started going around like a crazy man. More and more often people recounted how she would get up at night, braid her hair, and go from one garden to the next.

Alter's wife swore, "I've seen it myself, how she washes her face among the flowers at night. It's not for nothing her face glows like that."

And others swore, "She bathes in milk. Every night she takes a bath in milk. It's not for nothing her hands are like silver . . ."

The Archbishop

People knew an archbishop was coming to Skala, but they weren't making a big deal about it. It was only after they saw the pine-branch arches being erected for his arrival that they started talking about it in the street.

As redheaded Motkele, whose brother was a big shot over at the town hall, explained it, "Do they know their hands from their feet? They think an archbishop's just some other snot-nose kid! To rise that high? First he'd have to study to become a priest, because a priest isn't just born that way. Then he'd become a canon and then the chief canon, and then one of the elders, the rest of whom he's already forgotten by now. Oh, the lucky man. Then he'd become a bishop and only a long, long time after that would he get to be an archbishop."

Why an archbishop was coming to Skala, no one was really sure. Some-one said an archbishop came once every fifty years, and someone else said he came only when they built a new church. Henikh the marriage broker, who was standing nearby, took a look at the old church and mused, "That wouldn't be so bad; the town does need a new church." He spat sidelong, thinking to himself, "Just a nice new addition; then the town'd be more respectable, more civilized." And Henikh knew well how many matches were getting broken off just because Skala wasn't a civilized town.

In a word, as Henikh grew more and more attached to the idea, he started trying to convince everyone that this was the way it was, and it couldn't be otherwise. And the Jews began believing him, because when Henikh wanted to convince you, he pulled out all the stops.

Alter piped up: "So lookit, what's gonna happen with the town clock? What's everyone gonna look at?"

Truth is, Alter really wanted to get rid of the town clock. His place was right next to the Polish church, and given that he was a moneylender, he had nothing to do. So he spent the better part of his time staring at the clock. He was sick to death of looking at it because he felt that were it not for the clock he could have eaten his meals in peace, but the clock got him all turned around. For example, when he drank his morning cup of cocoa at around eight o'clock, he sometimes misread the time as nearing midday, which accounted for why he wasn't hungry and couldn't finish his meal.

Meantime, a couple of other people worried about the town clock. If it was taken down, they'd have nothing for their watches to keep time with since they set their watches to it. And if all the clocks in town went kaput, how would they know? After all, your time could run out without a clock.

Then Shloyme the deaf chimed in that it would be quite a boon, that it would bring prosperity to the town if they'd "'rect up" a new church.

"Prosperity from a church? How's that, Shloyme?"

Avrom the windbag took visible pleasure in having caught Shloyme's mistake.

Now, Shloyme was not particularly fond of having his mistakes caught, especially not by *that* one. So he responded angrily, "G'argue with y'rself, g'won!" Shloyme spoke with a broad accent because he was not a local. He said, looking right at Henikh, though actually meaning Avrom the windbag, "Why don't he unnerstand, eh? Dummkopf! When you 'rect up a church you need eng'neers—architects is what I mean—and workmen. The workmen they'll bring in from odder towns, goyim from the ends of the earth'll come to our fairs. Now does he finally unnerstand, the dummkopf?"

While he meant Avrom the windbag, he addressed his speech to Henikh the marriage broker, who understood but kept mum.

In a word, they started longing for the archbishop's arrival like they did for the Messiah (pardoning the comparison). Borukh promised Sluk the dowry after the archbishop came; and when Henikh had to pay his son's tuition, he begged Shloyme the deaf not to bother him till after the archbishop's visit, God help us!

A little later on there was a rumor that the rabbi was going to greet the archbishop while carrying a Torah scroll. A couple of curious people pounced on the sexton, Shloyme Perets, in the street, asking if it were true. Shloyme Perets winked his blind eye—the one that could spy a broken penny quicker than a sighted person—and mumbled in his nasal voice, "How should I know?"

"Up at the top of the street they're building an archway, and another one by the pharmacy. Dvoyre's standing right there."

That's what Godl reported to Alter, her father.

"What's Dvoyre doing over by the pharmacy? Tell her to come home and eat something."

Godl said she was standing there with Sheyndl, watching them build the archway.

"Well, if she's with Sheyndl, then that's all right. Sheyndl's a good girl." And with that he went home.

But now Sheyndl had already gone, and Dvoyre was still watching them build the archway. And in point of fact she hadn't even thought about Lutsyk. *So what if Lutsyk appeared on his own. If he appeared on his own, was that her fault? Was it her fault if they were building the archway right by the pharmacy? And if he said "good morning" and tipped his hat to her, was she not supposed to respond?*

"What a shame. So many pine saplings broken," Lutsyk said.

"Yes, a shame."

Should she not have responded?

When Lutsyk looked at her, she looked away.

She stood there a minute longer and fled. She felt the whole marketplace could tell she was burning for this gentile.

Then she felt the urge to head down to the wine taverns.

By the taverns she counted the saplings: one, two, three, four, five. "So many pine saplings broken."

A gentile was walking home to his village in a new straw hat with a peacock feather, playing "Hey, There under the Mountain" on a *drumbe*. The blue-green eye of the feather accompanied the song.

She felt a foreignness among the trees, with the gentile who was walking home by himself to his village, but she felt no fear. The marketplace and its stores, redolent with their Jewish wares, were calling her back.

*

Days passed, then weeks, and Dvoyre lived day and night with the words "So many pine saplings broken."

She felt sinful thinking about a gentile, so she dejectedly helped her mother darn socks. Her mother didn't know why, but all the same she didn't let Godl poke fun at Dvoyre.

Alter had been standing by the window, looking at the town clock, thinking about what he wanted out of life. When, for instance, it was eleven o'clock and there was still no roast, but it was finally ready by twelve. He argued that if only he might live long enough, with God's help, to see whether it'd be ready a little bit earlier today.

To which Breyne responded that all good things take a little effort, otherwise . . .

But Alter knew what she meant, so he interrupted her. Not a hint of steam to be seen on her; no fat dripping from her double chin. Were the dead to eat, that's the face they'd have. Did she hear him or not?

Of course she heard, and responded that he should set his mind to more profitable things. They had a marriageable daughter at home. Such misfortunes she endured.

Alter was speechless. But he didn't want to be caught flat-footed, "So she doesn't want Mayer Zisi. What am I supposed to do? And you, child, why don't you want Mayer Zisi, eh? Who are we supposed to talk to, girlie, eh? Who?"

Dvoyre was more than used to all of this. No matter where she went and what she did, people would mention Mayer Zisi: "Mayer Zisi's a good man"; "Mayer Zisi's a fine man"; "Mayer Zisi's got quite the Adam's apple and broad shoulders."

Dvoyre was used to her mother shaking her head: "It's really no? She really doesn't want him? What's she got to brag about—a girl's such a precious thing? Of course Mayer Zisi's got something to worry about; a young man's always got something to worry about. Such a sensible thing; couldn't be any more sensible. A sensible dowry here, a sensible dowry there, here a sensible inheritance, there a sensible inheritance. Our own cousins! What could be more sensible?"

But Dvoyre was used to it.

It had turned harvest time, and the cut wheat and rye lay in sheaves in the fields. People would cut across the fields of mown hay to go swimming, and the combination of the swimming and the summer evenings had given Dvoyre a tan. Everywhere she went Lutsyk's words followed her—over the footpaths, past the sheaves of wheat and rye, off by the mill—and she was ashamed to get undressed in front of his words. They dogged her, burning her shoulders, echoing her footfalls. *Wasn't her step beautiful? Graceful? Gazing into her eyes, weren't they beautiful in any mirror? Undo your braid, your long hair, Dvoyre? No, short braids are not beautiful, Dvoyre. Smear creams into them, wash them with yellow wildflowers, then you'll get long braids, long, long . . . And can you sing, Dvoyre? Then sing, but softer, softer, don't screech, that's unbecoming to a Jewish girl. Just a sigh, quietly, hush, to yourself . . .*

So many pine saplings broken . . .

The gentile was walking all alone into his village, going home, playing his *drumbe* so beautifully, "Hey, there under the mountain."

Convert to Christianity and die.

*

The following week, on Tuesday morning, Moyshe Yoyne beat his drum to let everyone know that the stores were to be closed. Whoever's shop was found open would be fined. That's how everyone knew that today was the day he was coming.

That morning Alter yelled at Godye that he dare not go because there was a rumor the army was going to be there and he might get trampled. Later, once the big to-do was already under way, he bumped into Godye again and yelled at him, "Go home! A Jew shouldn't watch such things. I'm going to the synagogue."

Later still, they chanced on one another again, right there where a Jew shouldn't watch.

The marketplace was packed with people. Now everyone would finally see that this was no simple affair. Yugan, the school principal, hadn't gone to spend the day getting drunk at mangy Moyshele's tavern, but instead, very early, when the cock crowed, he snuck in for a little nip.

All the gentiles who had come in from the surrounding villages were dressed in their Sunday best, and you could tell from looking at them that they were putting on airs for the great honor being done their town.

Dvoyre was standing by Hantsel's store, watching the circle of people formed by the police. Prokowicz was riding a horse and giving commands, his terrible policeman's mustache fluttering in the wind, a pine twig stuck in his lapel. Moyshe Yoyne the drunk, having hung up his drum, trailed along after him yelling, "*Nazad!* Stay back!"

When she saw this crowd of outsiders, gentiles all, in her Jewish marketplace, Dvoyre felt exactly like someone hosting a bunch of strangers who turn the house all topsy-turvy, guests who bring their unfamiliar things with them and stay for a while.

She was already looking forward to when they would head back into their little village hovels in the fields. Here was not theirs.

No one knew why they had formed into a circle; one jokester even swore that they'd made the circle so no pigs could get through. It was getting late and Yugan the school principal was still running around, bathed in sweat. Everyone was now watching the priests, fat and lean, tall and short. The loudest of all was the canon, who was the local priest. He had a face like a year-old heifer. His cook maintained he was an honest priest.

Suddenly there was some movement, some jostling, people jockeying with their heads, competing for space.

Someone announced that he was coming.

"Who's coming? Obviously the archbishop's coming; no, it's the rabbi who's coming, they're going out to greet the archbishop, right there. Stop it, quit your pushing, mister—I mean, Alter."

"Who is it, who is it, Reb Motye, can you see him? The archbishop—I mean the rabbi."

"Ho, ho, best say your 'pardon-the-comparison.' What a pip! An ox has got a long tongue and still can't blow the shofar."

"What's it got to do with you?"

"Quiet! There you go. Jews have found a good time to argue. Quiet, shush, they're singing. 'Who's singing? What's singing?' Are you deaf, or what? The sexton's singing. There's the rabbi with his retinue; there he goes with a Torah scroll. Itsik and Velvel are holding him under the arm. The sexton's singing. 'Shloyme Perets with the blind eye? What's the sexton singing?' It's the imperial anthem he's singing, the imperial anthem."

"Go on, Reb Alter! Let me have a look."

Alter didn't budge from the crate he was standing on. He just stood there. Even though he recognized Shloyme's voice, he pretended not to hear. "So what's there to see, eh? Never seen an archbishop before?" But a minute later Alter was himself so thoroughly astonished that he gave up a bit of the crate to Shloyme.

"Stand there. Easy does it, don't step on my foot. Oh, wow! Here comes the rabbi."

Dvoyre came running up.

"Dad, give me a hand up."

He made room so Dvoyre could watch.

The rabbi with the lovely beard was walking under a canopy, escorted by two respectable people carrying a Torah scroll. Four young men in silk kaftans carried the four poles that bore the canopy over the scroll.

Opposite them stood the archbishop—an old, grizzled priest, wearing a tall, angular hat. Walking next to him were young priests carrying crosses and wearing lace robes lavishly embroidered with silver. Two others in strange angular hats and white capes were carrying the crucifix.

When the rabbi approached the archbishop, both sides stopped. The Torah opposite Jesus.

It grew so quiet in the marketplace you could hear a fly buzzing. Everyone there—and they were as numerous as the sand in the sea—fell instantly silent.

Hush.

The archbishop bowed his head before the Torah.

*

"Ah, Jews, I can't bear it. The Messiah's on his way!"

"You saw it, he actually *bowed*."

"Of course he did, how else could it be? The Torah is older—*we* are older."

Dvoyre stood there as if in a dream.

If *they* walk over an iron bridge, they'll definitely fall in; if *we* walk over a spiderweb, we won't fall in.

She watched the old, stooped rabbi as he held the Torah, the Torah in its old velvet mantle embroidered with gold. The velvet and the gold were old and faded but distinguished and respectable like a wealthy old woman with a silk head kerchief, whose nobility and lineage were etched in the wrinkles on her face, in the dust of the velvet folds.

"My girl, why don't you want Mayer Zisi, eh?"

*

Word spread through town like good tidings: he had bowed, *he* had bowed. And when she ran off home, the words followed her: "How else could it be? The Torah is older—*we* are older."

Friedrich Schiller

"That girl, she's quiet as a dove. She knows all of Schiller by heart." That's what everyone said about Elka.

Elka and her older brother Asher were both soft-spoken. He was a bookish young man with a pious face. When their mother died, Elka had only just finished school. She took over the household chores. Her father, Itsik, was part owner of a timber forest. He was a kindhearted man, more learned than the rabbi (at least that's what everyone said). He was also vain. It was said he never remarried because no one was good enough.

All three were anxious, proud, and soft-spoken. If one of them wanted to speak, it was done bashfully, with downcast eyes. The siblings acted toward one another like two shy lovers. When a visitor arrived for the first time, the place seemed to him like a pious sanctum. With her white, aristocratic hands, Elka quietly managed the house and prepared it for the Sabbath. When she plaited the challah, her fingers made the same graceful movements as when she was braiding her hair.

All three of them sang beautifully. Their father like a clarinet, and the siblings like flutes; her tones higher and his deeper, but always soft, very soft. When their father began to sing the Sabbath hymns, Asher would accompany the cantorial tunes with his bass voice, while Elka, sitting apart in her room, sang along.

At embroidery class, all of the girls wanted to sit next to Elka. Somehow she held the needle differently than the rest of them. What she embroidered was *aristocratic, refined. Elka had made it.* Wherever she went, pride surrounded her. Anyone who got near her felt it; and what's more, pride suited her. The girls would sing German and Polish songs. But when Elka moistened her lips, they all grew quiet. They understood: *Elka was about to sing.* Then she sang one of Schiller's songs. But in her mind Schiller himself was the knight and she the nun who came to him in the valley. She always saw him, Schiller, lying bloodied somewhere in a field as she bent over him, dying with him, quietly . . . No, they got married somewhere off in a church.

From the moment she began to understand German he had been *her* Schiller. He became even more hers when she saw a picture of him with his aristocratic face, brocade down to his knees, and long stockings. She could not dispel this image all week long, though it was most difficult on the Sabbath—Sabbath morning, before prayers, when she sat by herself in her room reworking the braid she had washed the day before, in her cream dress and polished shoes.

That delicate Schiller with his songs and his entourage of young noblemen seemed to suit the quiet Sabbath in the aristocratic house and the proud girl with her freshly washed braid. The walls of her room, her little box of scented soap, the blue velvet ribbon around her throat were all suffused with his presence. She wandered around their home preparing for the Sabbath with this dream on her mind. She could have spent hours alone narrating Schiller's works from heart.

She made friends with the wealthy girl Babtsi Reyzis, and during the Sabbath the two of them would go for a walk past the town gate. There on one of the stone benches Elka would recount again and again the story of the beautiful Turandot and the princes who gave up their heads for her.

The one thing she kept to herself was what she thought about alone in her room before the Sabbath prayers. There they were, the young noblemen in their knee-length brocade and her bloody Schiller alone in the field, with whom she died quietly . . . No, they were married in a church.

During one of their walks they happened upon the count's young son with his pure face, dressed in green riding clothes, seated on a horse. Elka looked into his eyes and nearly fainted. From then on her Schiller wore the count's green riding clothes and the same pure expression as he bled alone in the field.

Just as the young count departed on a trip abroad, Zaleski returned home on school vacation. That's when he came upon the two girls out for a walk far beyond the town and followed them. At first they pretended not to see him, as respectable girls are supposed to do. But once the young Zaleski started to sing such beautiful German love songs, looking into their eyes and calling them *Liebchen*, their hearts exulted. From then on Elka saw her Schiller singing Zaleski's beautiful love songs, looking brashly into her eyes and calling her *Liebchen*.

Just as Zaleski returned to his studies, the mill keeper had a tutor brought in to prepare his children for the matriculation exams. The tutor could play the flute from sheet music and rode a bicycle. At least that's what Asher said, who was a friend of one of the mill keeper's boys. She once saw him from afar, and she blushed as she watched him bouncing along in his rakish cap. But since she was a quiet, respectable girl, she never saw him up close. Then one day Asher brought home a music book and declared with reverence, "It's the teacher's." And in one breath he told how the teacher praised his voice and was going to teach him to read music and sing.

Elka borrowed the book and shut herself in her room, taking in the designs on the cover and the scent of its pages. She went dizzy as the fragrance conjured the teacher before her eyes, walking daintily in his rakish cap, playing his flute. She developed a strong attachment to those sheets of music, staring at them endlessly until her bloody Schiller rose from the field and sped off on a bicycle, with a rakish cap on his head.

Later on, when there was talk of war, young people started crossing the border in large numbers. Among them was her cousin Arn, a boorish, uneducated young man.

Everyone whispered that he would be a good match for Elka—after all, he was family, and she had no dowry. However, Itsik felt the match was beneath their family; even his own brother's son wasn't good enough. What's more, the boy was poorly educated and, even worse, a Zionist.

Elka wasn't fond of this "Russian" either, but because her father didn't like him, she took the match more seriously. The relatives put the pressure on Itsik, yelling, "What d'you think, you're gonna get the Tshortkever Rebbe's grandson? Your own brother's kid—you should thank God for doing *that* well. If it wasn't for the war and all these young men, she'd never find a husband. So what d'you think? Bridegrooms are wandering the streets? No one's interested in a girl without a dowry. And so what if he's a Zionist? Everyone has faults; if it wasn't this, it would be something else." Itsik relented.

The marriage contract was drawn up, and four weeks later the wedding took place. Itsik set up the young couple in Elka's room, furnishing it with a kitchen.

Right after the wedding, Arn became something of a wheeler-dealer in the surrounding villages. He quickly lost his manners, forgoing propriety and boasting about business in his wife's presence.

Her father would sit at home for days on end, sick over the fact that this son-in-law, *his son-in-law*, had become a two-bit salesman. And what's even worse, Asher had run off to Switzerland to study the flute like some common entertainer. The house was fallen. The quiet, refined voices of this pure rabbinical family could no longer be heard inside those distinguished walls. Instead there was only the crude bellowing of this trader, good-naturedly cursing his ancestors.

Elka quickly grew fed up with this life. She wanted to return to her unmarried self. Babtsi distanced herself from Elka after the wedding— anyone could see how low she'd sunk. Then Elka's dream about her bloodied Schiller returned, but this time he was more mature, stronger. Now he was dressed in a black traveling cloak with a cape, seated on an Arabian horse, bidding farewell. She wandered aimlessly through the house like a stranger, ignoring her husband, quietly singing the songs of her childhood as she tied her girlish velvet ribbon around her neck and inhaled the scent of her shorn braid. She cried at length over these objects. After returning them to their chest, she would continue singing.

When Arn saw this little performance, he would grow frightened and say things like:

— "Have you lost your mind?"

— "Elsie, did something happen, God forbid?"

— "What's the matter with you?"

— "Why are you just sitting there singing?"

— "Who's that singing?"

Arn finally understood that she was longing for him but was too embarrassed to speak up. He sat down next to her, lay his hands on her wig, gave her a little slap on the cheek and whinnied, *hee, hee, hee.* Then his smooth yellow fingertip slid down her neck and throat.

She closed her eyes, wanting to deceive herself, and whispered, "Friedrich . . . Friedrich . . ." Arn reacted as though she were speaking to him: "What's that?"

But she didn't hear him and whispered, "Jump down from your horse . . . Don't go . . . Don't go . . ."

He responded, "Silly fool, who's going? Even if someone were paying my way . . ."

"Oh . . . Don't stare so brashly!"

"Who's staring? I'm not staring."

"Stare!"

"Now I'm staring."

She opened her eyes, her face waxen. Arn took pity on her. All she needed was some comforting and she'd be herself again. "I bought a calf today," he said as he kissed his two fingers. He patted her on the shoulder. "Elsie, it's as fat as you. That skinflint goy! Didn't want to sell for even fifteen guilders, the stubborn ass. So what do I do? Go ahead, guess. I sent in a buyer to lowball him and he gives him only nine, *hee, hee, hee.* The goy nearly died. A calf, I'm telling you. A Tyrolean. When the butchers saw me at the guard shack, they grabbed it from my hands. A Tyrolean."

Elka closed her eyes again, and there was her Schiller leaning over her shoulders with his pure face, saying farewell, calling her *Liebchen*, and speeding away in his rakish cap. Bloodied. All alone in a field. She quietly died with him . . . No, they got married in a church.

Another Bride

It was quite possibly the twentieth bride he been to look at so far, and as always it went like this. First Henekh the matchmaker would scope one out in the dry goods store and whisper his secret to old Hirsh. Then Hirsh would whisper it to Mrs. Hirsh, and she would tell it in strictest confidence to Sholem, their son. Nothing more was necessary. The whole town knew.

Sholem would be socializing with his friends, lost in thought, when someone would say, "I've got a secret," until everyone understood.

Sholem was no longer such a young man and it was about time for him to be a groom. But he wasn't having any of it—none of the potential brides he appraised appealed to him, and none met his impossible standards. Sholem, everyone said, wanted every strand of hair to wear a pearl.

He could hardly sign off on just anything; after all it was a bride he wanted, an educated one. He was himself a very small man, and his head sat on his pinched shoulders like a chicken in a basket, so he wanted a bride who was tall, beautiful, and clever.

People knew he was no fool and he acted the part. His memory was like a steel trap; he could list anyone's ancestry back to the fifth generation. If he read a novel, he could repeat the whole story with all the details, to everyone's amazement.

People found him very clever when he evaluated someone else's intelligence. If he called you a fool, no matter how intelligent you were, to the town you remained a fool.

The real reason he had not married was known to him alone. Quite simply—he liked traveling around looking at potential brides. It had become something he couldn't live without. There had been so very many young women he didn't want, but only because it would all end and Sholem didn't want it to end. He loved getting ready for the trip, the dressing up, the mounting of the cart, the commotion. Entering the potential bride's house where everything smelled of cleanliness and everyone was beautifully dressed, anticipating their joy. And the bride was radiant, awaiting *her* joy. There were pastries with preserves on the table, the brass samovar boiling, and a chicken roasting in the kitchen.

Thursday. The day of the fair. The store was full of peasants. He needed to go to Frenkel's shop to buy a collar. He set out into the street, taking another look at his mother standing there, surveying the merchandise and keeping an eye out for any peasants with sticky fingers.

The street was packed. He could barely push his way through. The fair roared with a thousand voices. The frost crackled. Peasants in gray sheepskin hats carried pelts, boots, fabric, new whips of braided leather. Peasant women were measuring out yards of linen, buying beads and putting them in their baskets.

Sholem pushed his way through the sacks of potatoes, the wagons full of cabbages and geese and chickens and ducks, unwittingly sticking his hand into a barrel of honey and wiping it off on a sack of corn. A peasant woman in a new floral kerchief folded around her face like a hoop yelled at him, but spun back around, the red cross flashing on her shoulders, because a customer had come.

Just then he noticed a small corpse being towed through the town. A small noble-looking corpse, and its mother, an inspector's wife, with her daughters, all walking in long mourning veils. Sholem glanced at the little coffin, with the small corpse, and at the long veils, and such long veils for such a little corpse didn't seem to him to be worth the trouble. The priest led the way in his white mantle, mumbling something that sounded like *"Hosti di bosti, hosti di bosti."* And the peasants carried large crosses for such a little corpse, and the deacon sang, for whatever good that would do, and the priest sang, for the fat lot of good it would do, and everyone sang.

It actually gladdened Sholem's heart—on account of a small corpse all of a sudden . . . *Wait, just a small corpse?—A corpse at all? When one encounters a corpse it's supposedly not good, they say . . . What is it that can't be good here? . . . At most it'll end up the way all the matches ended up . . .*

In the doorway of Frenkel's he met a peasant woman whose face was red from the frost. She was wearing green boots and carrying a white slaughtered piglet as big as a loaf of bread. Sholem took a look at the smooth white piglet, *it was so smooth, so well flayed . . . If you happened to sink a couple of teeth into it, right in the middle, sharp enough to leave deep marks . . . Teeth . . . Not his . . . Who's even saying they're his? . . .*

Henekh said she's an elegant specimen and was afraid the other side might want nothing to do with Sholem.

"The young woman you mean?"

"Well, well . . . Ultimately better not to ask . . . A princess . . . She but opened her mouth and pearls poured forth."

Henekh with his lies, he should drop dead—no, what he meant to say was Henekh should choke on the pearls . . .

He ran to Frenkel's shop and ordered a new collar with points *à la* Baron Hirsch. And as Frenkel was wrapping up the collar he grew increasingly anxious lest Frenkel ruin one of the points.

Later that evening, as Sholem was sitting in the sleigh with Henekh and his father, and the horses were panting, their flanks glistening, their ears pricked up, and their breath steaming out over the white road, Sholem kept fingering his Baron Hirsch collar to see if the points were lying even.

Despite the bitter crystalline frost, Sholem felt only warmth. The prospective bride, the princess, the one who when she opened her mouth pearls poured forth, was waiting in her warm rooms, where a fire was burning in the iron stove, packed with wood, and on the table stood the brass samovar boiling alongside the preserves and the pastries, and in the oven the chicken roasting . . .

His father, Hirsh, was sitting in a sheepskin coat, a leftover from better days, holding one hand in the other and telling a long story about how he had once driven his sleigh in haste to Czortków to get Doctor Shtekl—his wife had fallen ill.

"Well now, it was the end of the month, you couldn't see a thing, and what d'you know, I arrived at the station at almost the same time as the train, when all of a sudden the horse stumbled and drove into a post. There the sleigh stood, half on its rails, as the horse kept struggling back right into the sleigh's rails. And what d'you know, when I gave a firm tug at the reins at that very moment the train arrived. What could I tell you but if just another minute, another moment . . . What am I talking about, 'a moment'? It was the thousandth part of a moment . . . Let's not split hairs . . . That's why I'm not driving you Henekh, brother, to Ozeriany to look at a prospective bride . . ."

Henekh sat there leaning on his walking stick and listening to the story, not once interrupting, as was his way. He kept wiping the frost from his mustache with his red handkerchief, chomping at the bit to tell a story that had happened to him. Leybele the coachman, Moyshe the Beard's son, pricked up his ears; he spun his fur cap round and drove while seated askew, like he was one of the listeners.

When Hirsh finished his story he took a pinch of snuff, laughed triumphantly, and immediately indicated his desire to launch into a new story with a: "Quiet now, I'll tell you a better one . . ." But Henekh cut him off and started telling his own story. Only then did Sholem begin to listen.

Henekh was pleased as Punch they were letting him speak and grew more expansive: "Going with a wagon of geese from Czortków to Tulstenko, driving in and out of forests; Hirsh, you know how it is, traveling at night in winter with a wagon full of geese, you drive and you drive, driving, driving, and suddenly . . . Hirsh, just listen. As I am a father to my children and as I conduct my affairs honorably, I am telling you no lie; don't dismiss it, Hirsh, I swear to you by all that's holy . . ."

"Well, go on already, don't keep us waiting."

But Henekh kept them waiting till he uttered the word "wolves."

Hirsh and Leybele the coachman caught their breath—"wolves" . . . Henekh felt he'd let the cat out of the bag too quickly, that is, he hadn't kept them waiting in suspense long enough, so he wanted to get back to where he'd begun piling on his exaggerations: "So what d'you know, we had to throw them a goose, and then another. Well, did their eyes ever start blazing then. I tell you, they burned like candles, first two, then ten candles in a row. Did I say ten? Who can count?

"So, anyway, once they'd gotten a taste for goose they really started chasing us. We lit straw on fire and threw it into their path. The peasants crossed themselves—to no avail. We kept having to throw them another goose, which they'd pounce on. We could hear the bones cracking between their teeth. No sooner had we tossed them a goose than they'd stop for a moment, gobble down the last feathers, and start right up chasing us again. What d'you know, for as long as I live I won't forget that night. It continued like that till, till, till a mile before Tulstenko. We'd finally thrown them the last goose, all the straw from the wagon had been burned, and all of us, Jew and gentile alike, embraced one another. And they, the wolves that is, have no brains, right?—Yet when they sensed we were right at the edge of town they got even more brazen and simply ran after the cart. The horses were running like blazes. We had lit our last matches—till God rescued us! There was a cart coming toward us."

Sholem absorbed the stories, and he felt somehow even warmer. Now he wanted to encounter a whole pack of wolves so he could display his skillfulness. Then he would come to her, the princess, who when she opened her mouth pearls poured forth, he would come to where she was waiting, in her warm house, the samovar on the table boiling, next to the pastries and preserves, and the iron stove packed with wood, and in the iron stove a chicken roasting.

He looked out on the white road, at the trees that were bright with snow, and looked for a wolf. The frost crackled, sparkling as it lay on the branches. His father and the matchmaker gazed into the dark night swapping wintry tales of forests and wolves. And he, Sholem, thought of her, the prospective bride who when she opened her mouth pearls poured forth.

Viburnum

A fresh snow lay on the roofs, turning the town white. A wintry cheer shone into the houses.

Reyzl felt the urge to go outside. When her mother gave Hessi five kreuzer and a glass container to go buy kerosene, she volunteered to go instead. Everyone was astonished that Reyzl suddenly wanted to be a good girl. Her mother said something must have gotten into her.

It was the time for viburnum berries. The first, frozen berries. Peasant women put them out on the street to sell. And once the berries were glimpsed through windows, young and old alike scrambled from their homes to buy bundles of them. Bundles of frozen berries on beds of white wadding lay in nearly every window.

Reyzl had a strong craving for viburnum berries. When she thought about how their juice melted in her mouth, the little veins in her tongue contracted. She squeezed the five-kreuzer coin—she had to buy kerosene.

Outside there was a searing frost. The sun shone blindingly on the snow. She met some children, blue from cold, out to buy herring at the store. The smaller of the two limped behind because his boots were too tight for him. Itsi the glazier, his neck bundled in a scarf, carried a windowpane under his arm. The frost had made his sallow beard seem even more yellow. He was off somewhere to install a sash window.

Looking at his bundled neck made Reyzl sad. It reminded her how she was at her worst at home, unwilling to put a hand to cold water to help. At home they laughed at her, calling her *"gnädiges Fräulein."* If only she could keep from sleeping late, then Hessi wouldn't wake her with a taunting *"Gnädiges Fräulein,* I pray thee it's time to wake. Count Josef has already gone to church. At last you may now also get up." It didn't help if she pretended to be sleeping—Hessi knew. And even if she were actually sleeping, Hessi would still wake her up. In the morning, lying in her bed, she would think of the most wonderful things: a desperately besotted student, a lovely velvet dress trimmed with fur, dancing with a suitor in that lovely dress. But most of all she thought of running away to study in a big city, of becoming a doctor—*"Fräulein* Doctor, pardon me."

She walked through Khantsi's shop and noticed some fur trimmings hanging inside. There was a black Persian-lamb cap that would suit her dark hair perfectly. Her father was a poor man, and what with the brokerage not yielding, and she—well, there were two others ahead of her. After all, everything went first to Hessi, then to Rivtsi, and only then to her.

And if she stole it? It was hanging so low, and no one was watching. But it would be obvious to everyone. Her father would ask, "Where did you get that?" "Found it." "Where did you find it?" "Dunno." And then? Oh, how ashamed she would be. "Reyzele, a thief? Really? Such a quiet, naive girl. A respectable child, go figure." The policeman would walk her right into the town hall, with her father and mother following close behind. Her mother crying, her father biting his pale lips. Shame. Nothing but shame. And all of the town's children calling out, "Thief! Thief!"

No, she was an honest girl and no thief.

She went on farther up the street. She sensed people watching her because she was not yet an adult. She didn't stay at home, like a sensible girl, but was rather everywhere at once. She had ventured off to a far side of town and ran into a peasant woman selling viburnum berries. She felt her heart yearning for the berries. Because she wasn't an adult, her heart yearned as it did, craving something, longing both to break out of itself and not to break out of itself. *Why was she not yet an adult? Did she know why? How should she know? What did that mean anyway, "an adult"? It meant having to get up early, not thinking about lovely velvet dresses trimmed with fur; it meant washing the dishes and helping mother with her worries because there was no income. It meant pushing the desperately besotted student out of her mind, along with the vision of dancing with the suitor, becoming a doctor. It meant being sensible. Now it was about starting to darn a sock . . .*

Oh, how bitter viburnum berries were, how juicy they were. They were both good and not good. Her heart grew faint without them, and it grew faint when she had them. *Where could she get a kreuzer for a bundle of berries? She'd give her life for the taste of a single berry.*

She squeezed the five-kreuzer coin firmly, and her face turned red. She walked right up to the peasant woman and asked for five bundles of viburnum berries. The woman stood there, put her basket down on the ground, and chose out five bundles. Reyzl gave her the five-kreuzer coin that was now sweaty in her hand, and the peasant woman arranged the bundles into a bouquet.

When the woman had finally moved on, Reyzl was still standing in the same place. Suddenly she asked herself, "What have you done? And what about the kerosene?" But she drowned that out with other sounds so she wouldn't regret having spent the five kreuzer. "What're you going to say when you get home? 'Lost.' Lost and that's it. 'How does one lose such a thing? It would have been better if you'd lost your head instead.'"

She put a berry in her mouth. The winey, bitter juice felt cold as it dissolved on her tongue. They really did make the little veins in her tongue contract. She felt as if she were swallowing the clear frost, the cold sun on the snow, and all of it was like wine, dissolving in her blood like fire.

She had spent the five kreuzer. There would be no kerosene at home, and now they would have to sit in the dark. There were more five-kreuzer coins. Suddenly becoming a good child . . . Wanting to be obedient . . . She had never wanted to obey but now she did . . .

So why was her heart even more distressed? And the glass container for the kerosene. At least take home the container. No. Say that you broke it. With every berry she swallowed her heart endured that much more pain.

She plucked a berry from the bouquet of viburnum and swallowed it, agonized. She watched as the berries gradually dwindled, leaving only the thin, brown sticks, frozen, covered in snow. She felt sorry to tear them off, and with every berry it seemed like she was swallowing that five-kreuzer coin all over again.

Suddenly she noticed people looking up at the gate. People were making way; peasants were removing their hats. A dog was running out in front.

The count's young son.

He was all of eighteen, two years older than she. Just look at how elegant he was, how princely. Blond hair. Light blond hair down to his neck. Turning to gold, right at the neck. Gazing so proudly off somewhere in the distance, beyond the city. The city belonged to his father.

Her heart aflutter, she looked at the young count's hunting boots, which came up to his knees, at the gun over his shoulder and his game bag, at the lackey trailing after him.

She remembered her poor home and how today there would be no kerosene at all because she had lost those five kreuzer. She felt the urge to run after the count. To chase after him and his good luck, shining like a star in the heavens because he had been born a count, a nobleman's son. *He . . . Maybe he would fall in love with her? Maybe he would fall in love with her and carry her off into the forest away from her poor home? Into the forest on the hunt. Then into the palace above the gate, and then to Vienna, to court, to . . .*

Crazy.

She ran some way down the road past the shops in one breath, trying to catch up to him.

When she neared the church, she stopped to catch her breath. Her hot blood surged into her cheeks like two flowers, burning, prickling. She started walking in a dignified way, with measured steps in the middle of the street, looking down at the ground. She fanned the bouquet of viburnum in her hand, back and forth, back and forth. She felt the distance closing between them, and her heart started pounding more strongly. A pride suddenly awoke within her.

"Don't raise your head, don't raise it, don't. Don't look at him. But not to look at a nobleman's son? No, no, no . . ." She moved to the side and ran away. Then she regretted having run away.

"Whoever you are, *gnädiges Fräulein*, this suffering suits you, going out for kerosene and squandering, no, *losing* the five-kreuzer coin . . ."

The berries were so bitter. "What is he? Not as good a person as everyone else? Is he an angel? When he undresses . . . Hush."

His face sparkled like the snow. *It wasn't good there.* His proud gait bore him away, to some other place so that people might not be able to look at him, could derive no joy from it.

The viburnum berries gnawed away at her heart.

And what about the kerosene? What to do about the kerosene? It's already getting dark.

Why are viburnum berries bitter? And since they're bitter, why are they so good? And since my heart grows faint without them, why does my heart grow faint with them?

She wended her way back down by the shops, but her heart was still chasing after him, after the good luck that made him genteel, princely, so that his face sparkled like the snow.

Almonds

Hinde's hair was fashionably cropped. She smiled wryly at the customers in the tavern, her stylish bangs drawing everyone's attention. People considered her a free spirit. Everyone adored her, even those who hated her. Even her mother, the widow Gitl, would berate only Hinde's sister. All of her friends were crazy about her and would have followed her into a fire. Even her mother.

Who do you think was the first to get a Persian-lamb cap and collar? That Persian-lamb cap sure made her bangs pop.

In the evening, the musicians would assemble in the tavern before going off to play at some Christian ball. Hinde would come flying in with her short hair tousled, snatch up Mendl, the black tomcat, and start dancing a waltz.

She always kept her pocket full of almonds. The tavern patrons would whisper to one another that she stole money from the till. When her sister, Beyle, caught her eating almonds, she'd hiss through clenched teeth, "I really hope you get it for that."

As the days grew warmer, her mother said she was taking too many liberties. Ever since Hinde had made herself that bright muslin dress with the flowers, Beyle knew that Hinde would throw modesty to the wind and go off swimming.

Leybtsi was supposed to come over today to curl her hair. *He had promised.* Her mother and Beyle had gone off to Lashkowitz, and she was alone. She sang a Polish tune full of *I love you*'s, all the while watching out the window for Leybtsi.

Leybtsi. He had lived in Vienna, after all. A coiffeur. He had that smell.

The musicians Artsi and Velvele were sitting at a small table, cracking pumpkin seeds. Binyomin walked over to them: "Gimme a coupl'a seeds."

"Don't have any."

"Go drop dead."

"Yeah, go strangle yourself."

"I've got no energy to waste on you."

Artsi banged his fist on the table. *Dock-tock-tock. Dock-tock-tock.*

Velvele cried out, "Hinde, a pint!"

"Just look at him. He looks like he really needs a couple of bottles of Okoczymer?"

"Not used to anything else."

Ta-diddle, diddle, diddle, diddle dum, dock-tock-tock, dock-tock-tock.

Hinde brought the pint.

"Hinde, have you heard the new slang?"

"No."

Velvele gave Binyomen a jab: "So tell her."

"Hey, nice gams! Who's your mam?"

Velvele laughed.

Hinde responded, "That's the new one?"

She pinched Velvele's arm, a magnificent little pinch that jolted him forward and set him to dancing as she pitched an almond into his mouth.

"She's the living end. Just look at her crunching on those almonds. Stealing from the till, all while her mother and Beyle are away in Lashkowitz."

"She's gonna make it a Witches' Sabbath."

An inspector with fine blond hair and a mustache came in and sat down behind the folding screen.

Hinde recognized him as the new inspector from Nivre that everyone said played the fiddle.

"Miss, a serving of cottage cheese please."

When she brought him the cottage cheese, he wanted to sit her on his lap, but she spun away into a waltz and sang "The Carnival of Venice." He noticed how nicely her bangs fell over her forehead.

"Miss, come to me."

"Will you teach me how to play the fiddle?"

The look on her face dazzled him.

"Come home with me. I'll teach you how to play. You have such artistic hair—the fiddle will suit you well!"

"I'm coming with you."

She dashed out into the vestibule. Reuven, she knew, was going to be returning soon to eat his supper.

Reuven was the new son-in-law that her grandfather brought from Kolomea.

He was sitting on the bench; every day he came to his father-in-law's to eat his supper. He had such fearful eyes, watery and dark, like two cups of inky wine. *Why was he so frightened of her?* He was always frightened of her.

The first time he noticed the way she looked at him, he quickly snatched his eyes away and fled down the stairs. But little by little they got used to one another, each day stealing a quick look.

Today she would give him a good scare.

She hid behind the stairs. When she recognized his footsteps, she made a sudden move: "*Boo!*"

He noticed her waiting behind the stairs and spoke to the wall, "Why's she standing there, eh? She's got nothing to do inside? Just standing."

She jumped toward him and thrust an almond into his mouth.

He stood there aghast, her fingers on his lips. Then she ran inside.

Why did she always feel the need to look at him? She didn't know. She felt like she could just grab those eyes like two cups of wine and drink them down. And then? Then nothing, of course . . .

She went into the tavern and found Leybtsi waiting with the case of his curling iron and spirits and perfumes. He was going to curl her hair.

"Leybtsi, are you going to curl all of it?"

She handed him a couple of almonds, munching some herself.

Leybtsi followed her into her room and started curling her bangs. Bending over her, he held her short hair in his hands. She felt his soft, fragrant hand beneath her bangs, like a bottle of perfume trickling over her hair, her eyes, her mouth.

She grew tired of this pleasure, but let Leybtsi's fragrant hand continue to tickle her forehead, her ears, her mouth.

"Hindele, do you have a couple more almonds?"

Sitting on his lap, she snuggled up to him like a small child, her two fists at his chest, and leaned into him.

Leybtsi trembled. She felt the heat of the blood rushing to his face on her cheeks. *Oh, how it smelled . . . The blood smelled . . .* She snuggled up to him like a small child, wanting to drain the blood out of him, all the life it held.

Leybtsi picked her up in his arms and spoke as if deranged: "My luck! My luck!"

He threw her over his shoulder, and she held onto him with her arms around his neck.

"Are you going to take me with you to Vienna?"

There was a sudden commotion in the other room. Her mother had returned. She came into the tavern. There were gentiles who wanted tea with rum. Her mother groaned that she was exhausted from the trip. She berated the maid who was standing there, cursed Lashkowitz as well as the whole world for being full of nothing but thieves and murderers. Goodness gracious! She ordered herself some goose.

Hinde slipped out of her room and sat down in a peasant's cart. When she heard her mother calling her, she buried herself in the hay.

She came back that evening with a cluster of currants in her hair and currants in her ears like earrings.

The young men plucked the currants and popped them in their mouths. Hinde frolicked, as did her bangs.

More customers arrived, and all eyes sparkled at Hinde. The principal was there and so was the pale schoolteacher who wore a black cape and glasses. He obliged the principal, getting drunk so he'd feel more at ease.

She waited a minute till her mother turned around, then sneaked a couple of coins out of the till and slipped away. She went into Khantsl's shop through the back door and asked her to pour half a pound of toasted almonds into her pocket.

She took Bassi by the arm and went down to take a walk by the Zbrucz. It was already getting dark outside, and Hinde suddenly felt a pang of regret. She thought of Reuven, of Leybtsi. She felt as if something was missing, something was out of her grasp. This made her feel all the more guilty. Suddenly she heard a fiddle. *Oh! It's the priest's garden. The inspector lives there.* She left Bassi and jumped over the fence into the garden. The inspector was playing a song.

Hinde stood behind him, embarrassed. Was this the little inspector, the one who sat at the small table in their tavern eating cottage cheese and drinking beer?

She stood there embarrassed.

She would have hidden her eyes from anybody else, but she was willing to lean against his shoulders—one, two, one, two.

He looked around.

"Ah, Fräulein Hilda."

He was shy, she thought, unlike the others. She began to fawn over him.

As she sat on his lap, feeding him almonds, she tugged at his fine, blond hair. She wanted to catch the tune he played on the fiddle, but it had slipped away. It seemed to be hiding there, in those eyes, that fine hair, there in those lips, that soft mustache. She squirmed like a leech trying to draw the tune out of him. And then? Then nothing, of course.

The Pear Tree

Overnight the buds appeared on the pear tree. Even before then the birds could sense the hidden sap and kept whirling up and down the tree to see whether a leaf had finally sprouted.

In point of fact Leyzer had already noticed it, beginning maybe six weeks back, when the branches started forming little nubs. Leyzer thought about the past year and the many years before that—even back to when he had inserted the support stick, not yet knowing that what he'd planted was the cutting of a pear tree.

Leyzer had tended that little scrap of a garden since he moved into his own little scrap of a house. The garden wanted for nothing, since that poor couple had no children. But one mustn't sin against God's blessed name. That's probably the way it was supposed to be.

If not for that little garden, they would have had no consolation.

That garden with its little radishes and young potatoes. Leyzer's wife was famous for those radishes. When asked why her radishes grew better than anyone else's, Leyzer's wife would reply with concealed pride, "Practice." Ever since the tree had grown, it was as if a new consolation had come over them, God's goodwill. Leyzer loved that tree like his own child, and Leyzer's wife said, "He's like a devoted mother."

From the beginning he didn't want to believe it. Somehow the little support stick wasn't a normal stick; somehow the twigs were sprouting leaves, fresh young leaves. When he saw it was just going to keep growing bigger and bigger, he thought it would eventually obstruct the potatoes, so he wanted to tear it out. He pulled and pulled, but it was beyond his ability; it was something you needed a peasant for.

The little tree extended into the earth like, dare one say, a person, with all manner of roots and veins, large and small, clinging and entangling in the ground like a child in its mother's skirts. He took it as a matter of fate and left it alone.

But one time, when his neighbor Zaretski was passing by, he stopped and pointed at the little tree: "How'd you come by such a thing, Leyzer? They're real *Margaritkes*, 'daisies'! Where'd you nick 'em from?"

So Leyzer told his wife it was a pear tree, with real "daisies," and quietly thanked God for his goodwill. But from then on he started acting differently. He became a mean Jew. No, a *goyish* Jew. The kind of Jew whose children live in constant fear of him; the kind who always has his belt to hand.

He became a goyish Jew who guarded his tree with rigor. Woe to him who touched even a twig of that tree. Even a good friend once drew Leyzer's ire through the window: "You there! You, you!" Nothing had ever frightened that friend quite as much as that "You, you!" There was a hostility in it, a malice that chilled him. He felt he'd never been given a proper name and had rather been born a "You, you!" That "You, you!" burst forth like thunder, suddenly, unexpectedly, and jolted his heart.

There was no love lost for Leyzer in town, because he was such a goyish Jew.

The fact that the tree's branches had grown in through the window didn't seem to them a particularly Jewish state of affairs. And the fact that his face had grown ruddy instead of dull and sallow like other Jews estranged him even further. Even the great were wary of having much to do with him.

There were only two things he and the town needed from each other. He was considered the best craftsman in town. No one could make a trestle bed as well as he, so grudgingly people would come to him. In turn he needed them for the synagogue, where he had to go every Sabbath. *What would have been wrong with not going, God forbid? Was praying a torture to him? No, it wasn't praying, God forbid, but entering the little synagogue. No, it wasn't the synagogue, God forbid, but rather the people. When you think about it, what did they have against him? Did he take anything from anyone, God forbid? It was his toil, his effort . . . his blood. How many sleepless nights he spent fretting over a coming frost. Oh dear, the little tree will freeze. So he'd take some straw, and amid the searing frost he'd crouch down to cover up the little tree. Since he had no children—may he not sin by complaining—what else was there to do? But now, when it was all about to ripen . . . When the Almighty had shown a miracle and this very year there'd finally be fruit, everyone here was—well, they were conspiring against him, to ruin him. Take, for example, those jibes about renting that "orchard" of his, or other cutting remarks. Or take the fact that he hadn't been given a single good aliyah since three Passovers ago. Wasn't there a reason for it?*

Now, as soon as he'd seen the little green nubs on the tree, he went running in jubilantly to his wife.

"Pessi, it's finally happened! I've seen them!"

Leyzer's wife was astonished at him.

"Quiet, no Evil Eye. Don't talk like that, don't speak."

"But what does it matter, if it's finally happened . . . if the whole town sees."

"Well, let's hope it's auspicious. With God's help it'll rain. God in heaven."

Early every morning the two of them went out to inspect the tree. The poor things had no children, may they not sin by complaining. Over every new twig that sprouted on the tree they warded off the Evil Eye. Leyzer felt his heart growing healthier, and he kept saying to his wife, "This one right here, this one's worth any price, I swear."

As he stood with the plane in his hand, be it for a bench or a trestle bed, he took the wood and worked it as smooth as velvet. The shavings were as thin as silk and rolled off the plane like glossy white ringlets. But he was thinking about the tree. God willing, next year there would be so many "daisies," and the year after that, God willing, just as many. If a breeze should happen to gust, he would take fright and watch the branches: *They're swaying too hard, they're swaying too hard.*

On the Sabbath when he noticed the first fruits hidden behind the blossoms, he took his bench and stationed it outside the window. The pear tree's round leaves with their whitish undersides rustled in the warm breeze. He yelled in through the window, "Pessi, just come on outside!"

"I want to finish reading this week's Torah portion," Pessi said, appearing in the window with her glasses. "Get out of the garden; don't be so obvious."

Leyzer said, "Nothing of the sort. I'm going to bring out a pillow and a blanket and lie down for a spell by the tree. Come with me and sit down for a bit as well. This one, worth any price, I swear."

He finally grasped that Pessi would go. No, no, she couldn't. They, the poor things, had no children, may they not sin by complaining.

"Listen, Pessi, come here, a little closer. Where are you? Listen, since God has blessed our life, and the 'daisies' have just now appeared, I'll just go nail a couple of tall pickets on the side leading to the crooked street."

Pessi nodded: "Otherwise what, the one will outlive the other? You'll see—overnight they'll disappear and you won't even notice."

"Oh, I'll smash their heads. Just let them try to steal my pears."

Pessi straightened her kerchief.

"Ahhhh, the smell is such a pleasure. I've longed to add a couple of pears to my cholent. That cholent simmers something wonderful. A little bit of pear broth rouses the heart."

That vexed Leyzer.

"That 'ahhh' of yours, a Jewish woman will always be a Jewish woman. All you can think of is pear broth. Dummy, so you seem to feel what *that* is. Can you even grasp it? Pear broth. When it obviously moves your every limb. Why else would pears be important to me? The branches break, after all. It's a living thing, after all. You feel how it seems to sing along with my mood? Now my heart's filled with warmth; it sprouts, unfurls, leans in through the window and calls: *Come out, enjoy yourself, Leyzer. What do you have to live for when you have* no *children, poor thing* . . . Come summertime, and the sweat is flowing, and it's difficult to stand with the plane, it lowers its branches like a living person (you'll pardon the comparison) and despairs, awaiting a cool breeze. And it just takes a sharp whiff, sharing it with you. Then it starts fanning its branches in my face: *Here's a little breeze for you, cool yourself off, enjoy yourself, Leyzer* . . . Then come autumn and my heart's not well, it also stands there in a state of disheartenment, turning sallow, its health fading like a person (you'll pardon the comparison). When you go out at night during the penitential period before the High Holidays, it's been standing there for a long time already, groaning like an old Jew, same as you. Come winter and it's covered in snow, and it's cold outside but even colder inside—there it stands, the way one says, 'S'good in the ground, brother.' Pessi, what do you think, when for more than 120 years it's been this way . . . that there are no children."

Pessi stood up. "Are you starting up?"

Pessi was afraid to speak about *that* and always interrupted him when he did.

"You, you silly fool, what are you afraid of? We're not to that point yet, God forbid. We're just talking. Pessi, do you know what that smells of?"

Pessi shook her head.

"God forbid."

Shorn Hair

(A present for my aunt Zipporah)

Until Sheyndl was eighteen, her mother would wash and comb out her braids. Lustrous and thick, they grew all the way down to her waist.

From earliest childhood Sheyndl was a lovely creature. Her dress bore the whiff of her and grew as she grew. Her darning and mending were widely praised. What couldn't she do? She was the image of a bird in flight.

Her pious mother wouldn't let her attend school. After all, if Sheyndl's sister Nekhe hadn't learned how to write, she wouldn't have written those love notes to the examiner. But her mother couldn't take away Sheyndl's common sense. And Sheyndl had common sense. The fact that she was married off at nineteen to a sickly widower who died three months later—that was a bit of good luck. The misfortune came when that same year both her father and her devoted mother died, leaving her adrift with no support.

Sheyndl cried endlessly. She couldn't say what made her cry more: her two shorn braids that reminded her of her marriage, or her dear mother. Her room had been left to her as an inheritance. That poor little room without even a piece of bread.

Sheyndl didn't have a thing to eat. Her brothers were poor themselves. It really was generous of them—so they said—to let her stay.

When her mother was still alive, she used to buy a kreuzer's worth of squash seeds and wash them down with a draught of cold water; that did her a world of good. Now that a kreuzer was hard to come by, she had to forgo the pleasure.

She ran hungry to the cemetery and poured out a flood of tears. Were it not for Esther, God only knows what would have become of her.

Esther came from a respectable family. Since people have nothing better to do, they cooked up the idea that she was fond of talking with that young musician. Sheyndl knew it was nothing of the sort. If only everyone had Esther's character—toiling at her sewing machine and contributing what she could at home.

She wanted Sheyndl as a friend because Sheyndl was known to have a good reputation. And for her part, Sheyndl stuck to Esther because, despite what people said, she knew Esther was intelligent and respectable. She never told Esther she was hungry, because she was ashamed. Being hungry felt to her like a crime. *But what was she guilty of?*

Little by little Sheyndl learned how to sew. Eventually she started earning some money from it. No need to go about at loose ends anymore.

She started her own business. When she saw a whole florin in her hand, she felt she'd struck it rich. Straightaway a red satin apron took shape. A pair of gold-toned slippers with beads. A peasant blouse—bordeaux, trimmed with sheepskin—scented.

She was doing well, so people said, and a respectable girl.

They couldn't see how Sheyndl's heart wept within her. Each time she caught sight of her wig with the bangs in front, she felt a pang in her heart.

At night she stroked her bare head, back and forth, back and forth. Her hair grew faster and more lustrous. It felt to her like her two braids would *never* grow back. *And if they did manage to grow back eventually? Wouldn't she have to cut them off again? Again?—No. No? A Jewish woman, a wife? Woe is her miserable heart . . . No, God forbid! She wouldn't go around with her hair uncovered. Just under a wig. Her hair was already shorn. And why is that? Dear God, why is that? She hadn't even known her husband intimately; he was already sick before they got married. And her own hair?—God forbid! So what kind of sin would it be?—A serious, grievous sin . . .*

If only her braids would just grow back, then she'd feel at ease. She wouldn't cut them off till they'd grown out as long as they'd once been.

She kept the little house immaculate—the house she could finally afford on her own. During the day she would sit and work. At night she would clean until the place gleamed.

She wept over her misery. True, Esther was a friend, but a friend cannot be as deeply ingrained in one's heart as one's misery, one's sorrow. More than once her heart felt pangs of bitterness at the sight of Esther's hair. More than once she wished she could be an old maid, with everyone whispering about her in town, if only her hair were no longer shorn.

Her brothers spared no effort to marry her off again when they saw how well she was doing on her own. They would make a habit of visiting their sister at the gleaming little house, and over a glass of warm tea they would let drop, "What's the point of all this? How much longer will you be alone? One's supposed to get married, that's the way the world works." Her elder, pious brother argued that it was her duty to pass on to another generation.

At those moments Sheyndl would think of her growing hair. She felt as though they were after her life, that it really nettled them that her hair was finally growing back.

She would throw herself into her sewing and not respond.

When she was by herself again, she could feel the depths of her misfortune, *Oh, if only I could take those years back . . . Those youthful years . . . Old age gives you nothing but miseries. Miseries make a person—miseries make you old and gray before your time. Already thirty before you know it . . . What's the use when you can't get those years back? When you can't be like you were? Never exactly like you were. Can it be different? Perhaps even better? Better, better. Not for the sake of others, but for your own sake. You can be calm within, tranquil, joyful, not brooding. Only then you'll want to become more and more dignified. When you're dignified, you feel as if you're always walking around in a neat, new suit of clothes you're afraid to sully.*

In the gleaming little house stood a large mirror that Sheyndl polished with her dexterous hands until it sparkled like pure water. When she looked in the mirror, she saw yet another gleaming little house, another proper wife polishing another mirror, *and that wife was looking at her wig, and her heart was aching that her hair had been shorn so young, her years shorn away.*

On the little varnished table stood some glassware. A pair of majolica plates rested on a green stand, and a blue dish gleamed on the wall. There was a Turkish blanket lying on the bed, an expensive dress sewn by Moyshe the tailor hanging in the wardrobe.

Once her hair had grown longer, she started surreptitiously plucking a couple of strands at a time, and spinning and twining them into her wig. The first time she went out into the street, her heart nearly burst lest someone see. The next week she took a little more hair, and her heart likewise pounded. In this way, little by little, she took more and more hair. With her heart pounding and her body trembling, she waited to see if anyone would notice. Each time she appeared this way, a daring, new joy grew within her. She hoped that it would get better and better still.

Once, after Passover, the sun shone into her gleaming little house with such devotion that tears of joy welled up in her eyes. She looked out the bright window and rejoiced for no reason. That same day she pulled out all of the hair from the front of her head and wove it into her wig.

With a giddy heart she went to Esther's. On the way she met Itshe-Mayer's wife, who took one look at her and clapped her hands.

"Oh, good Lord! Walking around in your own hair?!"

Sheyndl stood there, not knowing what to say. Her heart beat like a bandit's. When she saw how terrified Sheyndl was, Itshe-Mayer's wife redoubled her fury.

"How can this be?! A Jewish woman, and the daughter of a pious mother to boot!" She kept hurling fire and brimstone.

Sheyndl walked back home crying. The day was so bright, which only caused her more pain.

Wine

All year long Mendel Kopils acted like a regular Jewish man. But when the two weeks before Passover rolled around, he would transform—you *had* to serve wine for Passover. Raisin wine.

Everywhere else people served wine during the eight days of Passover, but Mendel began serving it two weeks before.

The rest of the year his wife, Gitel, would buy raisins for the Sabbath, but for Passover Mendel would go himself to Dube's store to choose the best raisins. It was strange to see a man standing there, cool as a cucumber, sampling raisins.

For Mendel, though, the wine itself was the most important thing. Red wine and white wine both.

In town Mendel was considered a connoisseur. Everyone listened eagerly to the stories he told about old vintages. If anyone needed wine for a wedding or some other celebration, they would call on Mendel Kopils.

Mendel was a respectable man who traded beads and flowery handkerchiefs in bulk. He didn't interfere in the small shop where Gitel sold goyim cheap goods. He had his mind on other things. They had a girl of marriageable age at home, Tsiporah, bless her. He traveled constantly to see the Vizhnitser Rebbe so God might take pity and send a match.

That was the rest of the year. But when Passover came around, Mendel forgot about everything else. A day or two before the holiday he would go to Sanye's place to ask for a tasting. As the sip of wine entered his mouth, he would momentarily close his eyes and then, with a glance up at the ceiling and a gesture that signaled disgust, would say, "Bah!"

"Well now, Sanye, let me have some of the Bessarabian," and Sanye would serve him a taste of the Bessarabian wine. Again Mendel would close his eyes, savoring the wine as before, and say, "Well now, Sanye, let's have some of that Hungarian, the red." When he took a sip of the Hungarian red, his face softened, and he hesitated. "It's not quite right, but it's close."

Mendel was (God forbid!) no drunk, as the whole town knew and as Sanye knew. He was, rather, a wine connoisseur who constantly pontificated about how every wine had a living soul, some with a holy spirit and some with an evil spirit. It depended on what kind of wine it was. He didn't love wine for its own sake or for the pleasure of drinking it. It was for the secret that lay within. When he talked about wine, it was as though he was talking about something holy. That's why people loved to listen to his stories and why Sanye was always bringing it up in conversation. For example:

"Did you hear, Mendel, there was some talk today that if they reduce the tariff a bit, some better wine could be imported from abroad."

Mendel would wave his hand dismissively.

"You call it wine. They call everything wine. When my great-great-grandfather, may he rest in peace, called something wine, you knew it was wine. My great-great-grandfather was worthy of his merit. If you needed to see him, you first had to pass through a vestibule covered in copper, where, if you see what I'm saying, they counted the ducats for his company. You see, the count was a regular visitor. When the count needed to visit, it was, it was . . . What can I tell you, it caused a 'disturbance.' It was the count after all. Now one time, and you might want to hear this, Sanye . . ."

Sanye sat down to listen, and Mendel took a sip of the red, stroked his beard, brushed the whiskers away from his lips, and told the story.

"You might want to hear this, Sanye. It was on the eve of Shavuot, and one of my great-great-grandfather's daughters fell ill. What can I tell you, she was as radiant as seven suns, but it was fate. They brought the most prominent professors to her bedside, but it was no use—she was dying. By then it was the end of October, when suddenly the count pulled up in his carriage drawn by a pair of Arabian horses with shiny black manes. I'm telling you, those were fiery steeds. They couldn't stand still; they were of truly noble stock. They would have sold for no less than ten thousand. And the carriage, I tell you, it was . . . it was . . . Never mind. What's a carriage after all? Anyway, to cut a long story short, there was a cask of wine in the carriage, maybe a hundred years old. No lie. A hundred years at least. The count jumped out of the carriage and ordered that the cask be brought into the house, so the cask was brought inside. The count himself then went and poured a glass with his own hands and brought it to the girl. Well, did it help? As soon as she tasted the first drops of wine, she returned from death's door.

"You might ask whether the wine was kosher? But to save the sick it's permitted."

Mendel stroked his beard again and went on.

"Anyway, what can I say, what can I say. The wine had an international reputation. When given to a sick person—not much, mind you—just two drops and he's healed. Well, they only kept it for the sick."

Sanye had been hearing this story for years, but he still enjoyed hearing it again. It wasn't just the story itself but also the way Mendel told it. He would respond, "Yes, yes, those were the good old days."

"I tell you, Sanye, wine is like a good musician—you have to just let him play."

Sanye would always admit that Mendel was right, and that's why he let him taste liberally from every wine.

Meanwhile, at home, they had taken out the Passover dishes, and Tsiporah washed the bottles and cups.

The Passover dishes were an heirloom, and it's quite possible they came from his great-great-grandfather, who had brought them across the Black Sea.

The point is these dishes had a reputation in town.

There were valuable flowery bowls and platters, both fluted and smooth, which when you tapped them with the tip of your finger rang out like a fiddle string. There were plates so thin and delicate that when held up to the sun they burst with light like a ball of fire. The bottles were white and smooth and round with long necks. There were decanters, as lithe as ladies, with etched stoppers that sparkled like diamonds in the sun. The cups were real antiques. They were green, red, and blue, some with serpentine handles and others with narrow openings like cruets, and others still bloodred with golden flowers that looked like half-pints of blood.

The wine bottles were displayed in the window among the flowerpots. Tsiporah's flowers were famous. They all grew tall and full, just like her two red braids. Many people said the plants resembled her hair.

Tsiporah knew that she was a marriageable young woman; her father would whisper as much to her. She was already wearing the modest dress of a married woman. She was now the only daughter at home. Her two sisters had married in foreign cities and then left for America. That's why she was adored and why she felt so valuable as a potential bride. She began sighing like a bride, putting her mind to all the domestic chores and acting submissively to everyone. And that submissiveness felt sweet to her. Every Friday she would strain the raisin wine, then go outside and distribute the raisins to the children.

She loved the Passover wine bottles. Each person drinking a glass would toast her: "May God grant the speediest of engagements."

She would arrange the bottles of wine in the window among the flowerpots. When sunlight sparkled in the bottles, Mendel would sit in his home prepared for Passover, floors strewn with red sand, and look at the full bottles and the Passover dishes. He felt as though he were in a distant foreign land, where his great-great-grandfather had lived, where the vestibule was covered in copper, where they counted the ducats for his company, and where the count's fiery horses stood with the cask of wine in the carriage, and the horses couldn't stand still, chomping at the bit for somewhere off in the distance.

Like a child he would squint his eyes and look at the bottle of Hungarian red to see how the sunlight played in the wine, pricking it with its golden needles as the wine turned even redder. As he squinted his eyes further, the bottle began to elongate, to stretch out, to swell to an immeasurable size. There was an entire red world there, and he was floating inside of it. Now he understood the secret of what could return someone from death's door.

When he eventually awakened with a start from his reverie, he would spit, saying, "Bah! To hell with it," and then get mad at himself that he had let such foolishness into his head. And him a father with a daughter to marry off.

White Furs

Eight-year-old Brontsi would stand for hours near the border, looking out toward Russia.

The town lay on a hill overlooking a valley with a narrow river marking the Russian-Austrian border. If you stood on the mountain and leaned on the railing, you could see a large swath of land on the other side along with the red roof of the customs house.

Brontsi looked past the customs house, thinking of her rich uncle the wine seller, who lived there. She had longed to visit Russia ever since she first spied white fur trim on the Russian noblemen—in Russia they have white furs.

She had no mother. Her father, a merchant, was always off traveling through the countryside. His only child, she was often left with an aunt until he could return. There were more than enough children at her aunt's house, so no one paid any attention to her. She was free to run off and look out across the river. Ever since she learned that this was the border, she wanted to get to the other side. When her father came home from some village, she would play the spoiled child:

"When are you going to take me over there to buy a coat trimmed with white fur?"

"Soon."

"Daddy, daddy, daddy . . ."

"Crazy child."

She imagined that in Russia everyone went about in white furs.

"This Russia, what is it?"

"A country," her father said.

"A country, a country . . . with white furs."

One time a thick snow had fallen, covering the Russian fields on the other side. It seemed to her as if the land over there was an expanse of white furs.

That was in the winter. In summer, she was drawn to the water, to the border, because dark strawberries grew on that side of the river.

She often imagined her rich uncle standing by a cask, drawing off wine with a polished white glass and sharing it out with everyone. A good uncle shares wine. She wanted to visit him.

Every Friday evening she would follow the peasant carts loaded with flour as they made their way to the customs house. She would grab the coat-tails of Fishel, Basye's son, who took his cargo over the border every week. "Fishel, are you going across?"

"Go home or I'll tell your father."

"Give my regards to my uncle."

"What uncle? What uncle is he to me? Let go of my coat, you shameless girl. Go home, I'm warning you."

"He's the one who shares his wine."

She jumped in front of him like a clown. He couldn't get away until he had promised to send her greetings.

She longed to cross the border to Russia to see the white furs. When she started pestering her father, he would distract her with some little trinket, promising that he would soon be earning enough money so they could buy her uncle a nice gift. After all, it was impolite to visit without a gift. He was thinking the child needed a mother. Then he remembered the widow Pessi and gave a sweet sigh.

Like all orphans Brontsi was a wild child; she couldn't sit still. Her impulses pulled her from one place to another. As soon as she got there, she wanted to be somewhere else.

Her father traveled to Germany to sell oil. When he didn't return right away, people in town said he had disappeared. Some even said that he had died.

Brontsi went to stay with another aunt who had many children. This was no warmhearted aunt. She was constantly angry at Brontsi, looking for her every transgression: she brought food out to the dog; she didn't listen when someone sent her on an errand. Brontsi couldn't understand—*What was the problem with sharing food with Bosik? Did they need to yell at her? She wasn't giving away their bread—she was only sharing her own. She helped Bosik and he helped her. She didn't give or take a crumb more than was due. So what was the big deal? And she really didn't want to listen. Did she have to obey her aunt and do all her errands? It felt better to run off to the border and look across toward her wine-sharing uncle and the noblemen with their white furs.*

When her aunt realized that this would never stop, she cried to Brontsi's uncle, her father's brother. Her uncle, who couldn't bear to see tears, said, "I'm sending her over to Russia."

When Brontsi heard that they were sending her over, she danced for joy: white furs! When they seated her up on the cart next to Fishel, and the horse started pulling the wagon, a thrill jolted her, and she thought, "This is good."

After crossing the border, the journey finally started to tire her out. She gradually drifted off to sleep atop the wagon.

When she awoke in the Russian shtetl, and Fishel told her that they had arrived, she didn't want to believe him. She saw right away that here it was also right after the holidays, just like at home. People trudged up to their ankles in mud in the narrow streets. Little ramshackle houses stood by the bathhouse just as they did back home.

"Fishel, is this all of it?"

Fishel answered that that was all of it.

"So where are the noblemen with their white furs?"

Fishel laughed.

Fishel took her into one of the little houses. Inside there was a mud floor and a small glass case containing books. She went to open one of the books and saw that the pages were spattered with soot and gave off a musty odor. No, the odor was actually coming from the portraits of Baron Hirsch and Montefiore.

She was led into another house, where the tavern was located. There were long tables with benches and dirty Russians getting drunk and singing.

Her aunt, an old woman in a stiff bonnet whose eyes expressed nothing good, spun around with a large bunch of keys and swore at the servant girl. When she saw Brontsi, she didn't even kiss her on the cheek; she merely asked gruffly, "How are you, good?"

Her uncle, whose round face sported a beard that grew like a broom, looked her over. He ordered someone to give her something to eat with a voice that scared her to the point of tears.

Her aunt offered her a bowl of peas with some bread. Brontsi ate.

Meanwhile a commotion had broken out as one peasant slammed another onto the table, breaking a bottle. Her uncle came over and rammed his fist into the peasant's chin, bloodying him. The peasant burst into tears and sobbed drunkenly, "Berenyu, *za shto*—what for? Wh-a-a-a fo-o-o-o-r."

Brontsi's tears poured out just like the peasant's. She was afraid that someone might notice, so she wiped them furtively and went back to eating, swallowing her tears with the peas, every bite sticking in her throat.

Fishel was standing by the door looking around. She leaped toward him and grabbed his coattails, refusing to let go. He tore himself away. She hid her face in his coattails and sobbed, "Take me home, home."

Her uncle tried to convince her to stay. Her aunt made a friendly face and spoke with a kindly voice. She already knew that Brontsi was not going to stay.

"Stay here, dear, why are you crying? It will be good for you here. We can take you to the woods every day."

Fishel tried to help: "They'll buy you a little pair of galoshes."

Her uncle also tried to help: "We'll make you a coat."

Teary eyed and whimpering, she asked, "Trimmed with white fur?"

Her uncle smiled, and everyone laughed. Then her aunt said, "Of course, my dear, what else? As long as you stay."

But she understood that it was all a lie. There were no white furs. When you get hit on the chin, your blood flows and you cry. It was terrible there. The peas choked her, and a new lament came out: "Home, I want to go home."

When Fishel saw how the child clung to him, his heart wept. He stood there confused. Her uncle said, "So be it, you can see she doesn't want to stay. Enough. Take her home."

When she was finally seated next to him on the cart, with her aunt and uncle standing by watching with folded arms, she suddenly felt a love for them because she could leave them behind, and shouted, "Goodbye, goodbye!"

But on the other side of the border, as they traveled uphill toward home, she began to feel regret over something.

Fishel asked her, "So, do you think you'll want to go back to Russia? I told you, didn't I?"

She sat with her broken heart and cried. Not because her aunt didn't let her give any food to the dog, and not because her aunt had made her do errands, and not even because her father had disappeared somewhere, but because over there, there were no white furs.

Cholera

Early one morning people learned that cholera had come to their city. How did they come to learn that? Because at Moyshe Libes's place, may it never happen to you, they were all laid up in bed. How did people know it was cholera? The doctor said so. And if the doctor had *not* said so, wouldn't people have understood it on their own? Why did they need the doctor to tell them? That "Viennese" doctor, that "simple Shaye-Moyshe," hasn't got a clue. Where did it come from? They had gorged on spoiled fish. Well . . .

But everyone kept pestering the Viennese doctor: "Herr Doctor, what do you say? Is it cholera?"

Everyone who had been calling him "Shaye-Moyshe" behind his back blanched when that Viennese doctor walked by, snatching off their hats and taking their yarmulkes with them, bowing and smiling: "Herr Doctor!"

Yitskhok was brazen, more brazen than anyone else. He made fun of the Viennese doctor more than the rest. "He's a simpleton, knows even less than a Shaye-Moyshe. He's a shoemaker, not a doctor. You ever seen such a doctor? He writes the same prescription for everyone!" Yitskhok's son Berele could read—he was in the second form in the gymnasium after all. On every prescription he read the word *Aqua*. "*Aqua* means 'water.'"

"Well, that's all good then, Reb Yitskhok. Why are you making such a fuss? If it's called 'water' then it's obviously some sort of tincture, and there are all kinds of those."

That's how Moyshele stuck up for the doctor, though people said that his wife and the doctor . . .

Yitskhok understood, but for appearances' sake he pretended not to know. What did it matter to him what people said? He responded to Moyshele only that there were also pills and ointments for every illness in the world.

The Jews argued that "Shaye-Moyshe" was going to ruin the town: there was *cholera* going around, and he said it was nothing.

But when the doctor walked down the street with his Germanic "Herr Doctor" gait, administering nasal doses of phenol and other medicines that all smelled like his suit, a couple of Jews moved to the side so as not to block his way and to let him pass by with greater ease. The rest of the group stayed put. You may ask why they made a point of standing on *that* side? Why shouldn't they stand on that side? Was it their fault if *he* was trying to walk through *their* group?

When the doctor didn't stop, they anxiously pushed him right into the street with a "Herr Doctor."

The most brazen among them, Yitskhok was somewhat unsettled by this, and his face started to color. As he became more flustered, he flushed fully crimson.

The doctor was indignant. These people were deranged, and Skala was such a strange town. It was the first time in his life that he had experienced such a fanatical place. He told them over and over again that it was *not* cholera, and *basta*!

The doctor left with his Germanic "Herr Doctor" gait and with the distinguished odor of the phenol and other medicines. Not cholera!—go try and stop him.

It did actually vex everyone quite a bit. Zishe the teacher said with that voice of his like a clay pot, "What does that mean, 'it's not cholera'? Jews, it's gonna ruin the town! Why are you silent?"

"What can we do?"

Everyone got good and mad at the doctor, especially the farther away he got. Then Yitskhok really let loose: "Such a Shaye-Moyshe! Y'ever seen such a doctor? Who asked for a disaster like that here? What, you think he was gonna do right by little old Skala? Obviously the town was never gonna please him. Came with only a single pair of trousers."

In town it spread as quickly as fire as people whispered to one another, spitting as they said their *May it not happen to me*'s and their *May it not happen here*'s and their *God forbid*'s.

The Jews never kept quiet. Here's the proof: the town hall dispatched a peasant with a pail of white paint. The peasant painted Moyshe Libes's filthy gate with white lime, sealing it shut. Then both of the town's policemen—Prokopowicz and Moyshe-Yoyne—were stationed on either side of the gate to guard it, letting no one in or out. A liter of carbolic acid was poured in front of the gate so that all the pigs fled the street. That evening the drumbeat went out that there was cholera in town and no fish could be purchased for the Sabbath.

When the Jews who had caused the whole ruckus in the first place took a look at Moyshe Libes's gate—as big as a tavern's it was—well, when they took a look and saw it painted white, terror descended on them. That white gate right in their midst was worse than cholera itself, because their houses were just as houses were supposed to be: dirty, spattered with mud, their walls peeling down to the clay, their roofs more or less as roofs are supposed to be. Now all of a sudden here's your catastrophe: a white gate!

Now when the doctor arrived, everyone hustled off to the side. They were afraid lest they catch it. They exchanged whispers with whomever they met about whether someone had caught it. They talked about this person and about that person. But then it turned out that both this one and that one were well and healthy.

There were two things people kept an eye on the way they watched for a fire: namely, fish and the street with Moyshe Libes's white gate. When people spied a peasant with a basket of little fish, the market vendors all made a hue and cry and drove him away. A great many housewives threw out their fish pans in the cemetery. And if someone even so much as mentioned Moyshe Libes's white gate, they were given a ten-foot berth.

One thing was strange, though: why wasn't anyone dying at Moyshe Libes's place? For the moment there was no word that anyone had died there. They waited and waited; a day, two days, three—no one dead. The doctor came and went as usual, as if it were nothing to him. He walked with his Germanic "Herr Doctor" gait, as if to say, "Mangy wretches." When someone stopped him with a "Herr Doctor," he'd let loose his indignation with his customary "You're all crazy. It's not cholera . . . *basta!*"

It had become a matter of spite. People kept watch to see whether anyone had died at Moyshe Libes's just so that the doctor himself should know what a Shaye-Moyshe he was.

But when *no one* had died at Moyshe Libes's place, people actually started getting irritated. "How much longer is this suffering going to go on? Among respectable people cholera takes a day, maybe two, and that's the end of it. And here's it's been three days already and you don't see or hear of anyone."

Suddenly, around Thursday evening of the fourth day, people were astonished to see Moyshe Libes in front of his gate, standing there dressed, smoking a "seegar" and smoothing out his beard as if it all had nothing to do with him. *Well?*

The town was utterly bewildered. To go and get up after cholera, healthy, dressed, so that anyone might catch it. Pshaw. They were ready to tear him to bits. The first one to notice was Leybele the butcher's son. He pointed it out to Zaynvel, and soon there was a flood of children gawking. The policemen were not stationed on guard. Apparently someone, if not the doctor himself, had dismissed them. And the gate, the white-limed gate, stood open—open, ready to let the cholera out into the town. When they saw the open gate, people grew even more terrified.

Sabbath morning in the marketplace people saw Moyshe Libes's entire family, the ones who had been laid low with cholera, all hale and hearty.

They had dressed up, as if out of spite, wearing their Sabbath best, alongside all of their relatives, aunts, cousins, and sisters-in-law, standing there none the worse for wear. People were perplexed: "What does this mean?"

By the next week the white gate had already been bespattered with black mud, and Moyshe Libes strolled free and easy down the street. When he walked through the group in which Zishe the teacher was standing, Zishe ignored it and instead asked him with that voice of his like a clay pot, "What was the matter with you, Reb Moyshe?"

"You mean you don't know? The cholera, may it not happen to you."

Zishe was annoyed by the pride with which Moyshe had said "cholera." He envied him his cholera and gave him a look as if to say, "So why are you still alive?" He repeated with a particularly Jewishy smile, "The *cho-le-ra*? Y'know what that stinks of, Reb Moyshe?"

Moyshe answered with even more pride, "Do I look like I know?"

It really irritated everyone that he should be enjoying himself so much. Yitskhok said it was probably just the start of cholera. Leybele said it wasn't even that but just a severe inflammation of the gut. Zishe the teacher, now good and angry, responded that it wasn't even a gut inflammation, but rather it had to be simply indigestion.

A Spa

Every little thing made Itte mad at her husband. And when Itte got mad at her husband, it caused him no end of grief, because Itte was not one to just kiss and make up. When Itte got mad, she stayed mad for at least a week.

Mostly she got mad when Yankl refused to get her something that Mrs. Ehrenberg had and she didn't.

In town they said that Itte was always cozying up to the wealthy Ehrenbergs. She copied everything Mrs. Ehrenberg did and went so far as frequenting the same doctors. She even considered it an honor not to have any children because Mrs. Ehrenberg also had no children.

When Yankl learned what people were saying in town, he scolded her: "Why do you have to go visiting Mrs. Ehrenberg every Sabbath? Why doesn't Mrs. Ehrenberg ever come see you?"

Well, that was all it took: Itte lowered her nose, screwed up her face, and barely an hour later was laid low in bed, racked with spasms. That's how it always was when she got angry. First came the spasms. Then, when it got bad, when Yankl came to check on her and there was no one to cook his kasha and broth, and he had to set the table himself, that's when he started circling the bed, meaning he wanted to make up. But what did it matter what he wanted, because that was obviously not what she wanted. She wanted to teach him a lesson yet again. So the first day she wouldn't respond to him at all. But the next day, when he had given in to whatever *she* wanted, she'd start speaking about him loudly enough for him to hear through the wall: "Let *him* go take care of himself, let *him* go set the table. Oh, woe is me, misery and despair are my life! My enemies should have as much strength to breathe as I do to move. Let *him* go pour a cup of soup for dinner. What's he doing just standing there like a dumb clod?!"

That meant things were good. When Yankl finally heard those words, he was beside himself with joy. When she called him "dumb clod," it meant she'd soon be on friendly terms again.

Itte was resolutely self-possessed. Given that he still hadn't divorced her after ten years of marriage, she felt she had the upper hand. From year to year she relished keeping him confused. And even if Yankl had from time to time given a thought to being free of her after ten years, even if he had indeed wanted to give it a thought, he simply couldn't. He didn't have the time. When would that be anyway, when her spasms took up all of his time. Of course, he was wholly committed to making up with her. But how, for example, could he find the time to make up with her when he was so busy cooking his own kasha and broth?

Yankl was a Vizhnitser Hasid and Itte had wanted him to become a Tshortkever Hasid, so when they were younger they were at each other's throats. Why had Itte wanted him to become a Tshortkever Hasid? Because barren women were "helped" by the Tshortkever Rebbe. First *that* one is being helped, now *this* one is being helped by the Tshortkever Rebbe. Even though that Yisroel was still a fairly young man and had nowhere near the accumulated divine merit of the old Vizhnitser Rebbe, still you could be helped more quickly by the younger rabbi, Yisroel . . .

For his part Yankl knew she was right. He also knew of a lot of women who *were* helped by Yisroel when the Vizhnitser Rebbe couldn't help them. Take Gitele, for example, the Vizhnitser's own relative, right?—the grand-daughter of either a cousin twice removed or a third cousin—and *still* the Vizhnitser could accomplish nothing. When it came to children, he was no hero. By contrast, nine months on the dot after Gitele went to Yisroel. Everyone in need should be so lucky.

What else was there for it but to go and become a Tshortkever Hasid?—May his enemies not live long enough to see such a thing. His father would be rolling in his grave. What's more, it posed a danger, a mortal danger: he'd promised his father on his deathbed that he'd remain a Vizhnitser.

She wanted to go see the Tshortkever Rebbe, so he let her go see the Tshortkever Rebbe. *So when it wasn't successful, was it his fault? You see? Apparently she blamed him. It wasn't successful because he, Yankl, wasn't a Tshortkever Hasid! But what does it matter what she said? Should he go and make his life that miserable? No! Not that!*

But he did other things for her. You might ask whether or not the interest he dealt in yielded much profit? But still, when she wanted to keep up with Mrs. Ehrenberg, with this bauble or that hat or that wig, for example; when she wanted to imitate her style and every day put on the same wig as Mrs. Ehrenberg; when she didn't want to go around in a kerchief like all the other women, but instead in a wig like the rich folk. *Why should he kill himself over it? He had other things to worry about. He had business he preferred to attend to. His brain was going to shrivel—may the anti-Semites be similarly afflicted—from a rather more important matter: they were going to go entrust the synagogue trusteeship to Notl. Notl, who was a heretic and a bastard to boot, was going to lay waste to their Jewishness, that heathen.*

Who didn't know that Notl had secretly converted? Take as an example—just listen to the chutzpah, the outrage this shegetz, *this non-Jew, can commit out of spite—take as an example the* mikveh. *You're supposed to flush the* mikveh *twice a year, not once because you feel like it . . . Just listen, I'm asking you, to what a miscreant like that can do just because he feels like it . . . But Khanina gave him a good what for: "When you feel like it you can grab someone's nose like this . . ."*

As for Itte, his anger had no intention of letting up. *Make up your mind: You want a new hat? So buy yourself a new hat. A new wig? Buy yourself a new wig. As long as you leave me alone, let that be the end of it.* He had just given in to her when she spoke to him again through the wall with her "just let him," put on a cheerful expression, and called him "dumb clod." It seemed she was on the verge of returning to friendly terms. But looks can be deceiving! A whole day he spent circling the bed where she lay moaning. He was seriously frightened: maybe she really wasn't well?

He came closer.

"Itte, maybe I should call the doctor?"

Itte groaned that she could feel a stone and said to him "through the wall": "I don't need him. The doctor can't help me."

"So what can we do? Maybe a little hat?"

Itte burst into tears. "So many miseries I have to suffer! I don't even have anyone to pour my pain out to. What I'm missing's not a little hat. He thinks it's nothing, that's what he thinks. I'm not afraid, you'll—it'll beat its way into his heart yet. He feels nothing. He thinks an angel's toying with him. I'm not afraid, he's got enough on his plate, enough to worry about."

Yankl was scared to death and interrupted her: "Itte, what's going on?"

"What should be going on? The miseries I endure and the grief I suffer! That's all of it, and he asks what's going on."

"Itte, for me, please, live a long and healthy life, if only you'd just tell me what's going on."

Itte grew frightened at the fact that he was frightened, and when he saw her afraid, he got even more scared.

"Itte, may you not die young. Just tell me what's . . ."

That oath finally seemed to have helped, because Itte was afraid of dying young. The closer she got to fifty the greater her fear of an early death. That's why she would swear, "May I be preserved from an early death."

Now when Yankl raised the specter of dying young, she was terrified.

"Madman! Just look! Why are you scheming against me? You're scheming, don't you see? May such ill befall my enemies' heads! Their hands and feet! Their bodies and souls!"

"Itte . . ."

She was afraid he'd raise that specter again and cut him off: "I should have . . . *ahem, ahem, hem, heh heh* . . . Oh, the pain's stabbing me in the shoulders. Do I even have one bit working in this miserable body? If I went to see some great professor, my case'd confound him, oh! But that's no matter when I've got someone like Yankl Bunzi's to consult. Here, among respectable people . . . such as Mrs. Ehrenberg."

Itte sat up in bed, trembling.

"Respectable people like Mrs. Ehrenberg, they go to a spa . . ."

"So that's it . . . A *spa* . . ."

"A spa, yes, a spa."

"A *spaaa* . . ."

Yankl couldn't snap out of it. He never expected such a shock. He just kept drawling it out: "*A spaaa* . . . Mrs. *Eeeh-reeen-beeeerg* . . . she's going to a spa? Mrs. *Eeeh-reeen-beeeerg* . . . Who can compare with Mrs. Ehrenberg?"

Itte kept trembling.

"Well, what do you think when one's leaving this world so young. Oh! The spasm's come back. Oh!"

She fell back in bed as if paralyzed.

And Yankl thought, *Spasms—that's bad.*

"Tell me, Itte. How much do you think that would involve, this spa?"

Itte frowned.

"Let me see. About a hundred and fifty or two hundred florins."

"Ahhhhh . . . Two hundred florins? Ahhhh . . ."

But when he noticed her moans getting louder and her eyes shut, he understood that the anger would be prolonged and extensive, so he caught himself.

"Itte, when's she going, Mrs. Ehrenberg?"

Itte groaned weakly, "The Sabbath after Shavuot."

Yankl stood up.

"The Sabbath after Shavuot? Well, let's see . . ."

AMERICAN STORIES

A Cut

People are strolling in and out of the park, each and every one of them taking even strides, while May limps *just* a little.

It's hot. The white clothing and floral hats intensify the heat. Hearts burn for cool water, for flirtations. They burn with longing to fly far away to some unknown hideaway.

They burn with longing, and it makes one ashamed to look them in the eye.

May had sewn her own dress the day before. She had tried it on maybe fifteen times because one end of the collar was an eighth of an inch too long. *Who would notice what a serious effort it took to make the ends of the collar even?*

Today she went to see Annie to ask if she wanted to go to the park with her. *Why shouldn't she go and ask Annie? She'd hear excellent music there, classical music.* Annie said, "Classical music?" and still didn't feel like going. May had barely dragged Annie out last Sunday, after May had spotted a young man through the window. *Was it so terrible that she dragged Annie away? After all she had spent half the summer sitting at home, and no one asked her out. People did come to visit her. Isn't she educated and clever and a good conversationalist? But no one wants to go out with her—she limps a little.*

For the music. That's why she has gone to see Annie. Come now, what's so urgent? To see Waldman?—Nonsense!

She went to see Annie, and she knows Annie's parents aren't happy about it. Different young men are always coming to May's house and then nothing, neither seen nor heard from again. Even that Waldman, the penniless "writer," whom people took it upon themselves to feed, even he eventually cast her aside, can you imagine! *Was this an appropriate example for their child?*

May knew what they were thinking. But after all, that limp had been of some use to her. It had certainly sharpened that mind of hers and put it through its paces.

While Annie stood indifferently in front of the table, asking May to wait until she had something to eat and saying she did feel like going and then she did not feel like it anymore, and when Annie's father asked, "Where are you going? Where, I'd like to know," furrowing his brow, as if May were going to corrupt Annie, May's blood drained from her face. Still she stood there joking and laughing, and she gestured with her hand against a glass next to the knives and spoons and forks, a gesture that made her finger hit the knife blade, causing her blood to flow for real. She didn't make a big deal of it. She went on laughing, despite the distress in her heart. But when the others got frightened and started dousing her with peroxide, she knew the wound was actually in her heart, not her finger, and no dressing could stop that blood from spilling.

And all this because she limps just a little . . .

Now she treats Annie like a treasure, as she drags her to the park. *One must be stubborn to achieve one's goals, to be nobody's fool.*

They arrive at the statue of Beethoven. As the pleasant swells of music hit them, they both ask at once, "What are they playing?"

If she could just extend her foot a little, just a little, her left heel would reach the ground completely. She hasn't exercised putting that foot down enough. And she is responsible for that. This is an example of her life, just a little one.

With a smile May pulls out the program she had gotten from a neighbor. The neighbor had told her, "They'll be playing *William Tell*."

"*William Tell*?"

Waldman stands there between a couple of girls. Waldman—"My dear Miss, a poet cannot become attached to one woman."

Those girls have been standing there by the statue of Beethoven for five years already, waiting for a husband . . . just like her.

No, not like her . . .

They doused her with peroxide.

There were so many forks and spoons, and she found the blade of a knife. Just the blade of the knife she needed to find.

"*William Tell* is lovely!"

"Yes, *William Tell* is lovely!"

Of course Annie is thinking about the young man who might show up there today. Annie is an ignorant girl, who can barely sign her name. But even she can feel the music in her head.

Oh, May understands what Annie is thinking! But after all, that limp had been of some use to her. It had certainly sharpened that mind of hers and put it through its paces.

"*William Tell* is really lovely!"

May looks at the text of the program for *William Tell* and thinks about how much more lovely it would be to sit in a field somewhere with a faithful dog and have a good cry about something.

How many forks and spoons there were, how many forks and spoons, and then the blade of a knife.

That dog should lie quietly in the field and not speak any fine words of consolation over the fact that she limps a little.

They doused her with peroxide.

And let the earth be calm and quiet, and let its grass grow tall and soft so she can cover her bare feet in it, the foot that limps a little, and cry softly.

Waldman approaches.

"Oh, how interesting you are today, the devil'll get you for it!"

And she smiles coldly, but her eyes, embarrassed by their own happiness, look to the side. They look to the side and defend themselves against everything they find: "We are not responsible. We didn't come here because we wanted something. We don't want anything . . . We just want to go cry quietly in a corner. No, we don't want to laugh . . ."

Waldman regards her with the look of one who has just read *The Ego and Its Own* and *Zarathustra*. It is a forceful, "compelling" look.

To Annie he also pays a compliment, and Annie smiles. Then he turns back to those girls.

And the music scolds, rises into the air and threatens, gnashing its teeth and suppressing its fury.

But from time to time a quiet voice, a sob, breaks through: "Only a little cut in my finger, only a little cut . . . But I'm not crying, I'm not crying . . . *William Tell . . . William Tell . . .*"

The First Patient

When the new dentist, Turner, a young man of twenty-one, received his first patient, he became flustered, turned red, and spoke too much. His parents were sitting in the waiting room watching. After working so long for that diploma, they wanted to get a little joy from it.

Turner guided the patient—a middle-aged woman—into the private exam room, sat her in the chair, and closed the door behind him.

When the dentist's mother heard the patient in the other room, she actually leaped up from her seat and blurted out, "A patient!" Her husband restrained her: "Shh, sit still." And when she couldn't sit still and went to have a look through the crack in the door, he got angry: "Stop running around like that—you'll frighten the patient."

When their son came out to get something, the two of them stood up.

"Who is it?"

"A patient."

"What does she want?"

"A tooth pulled."

The father moved closer to him. "Look, son, this is it, your big chance."

The son was offended. "Papa, what's the matter with you?"

"No, don't be mad. I won't say any more: just be careful."

"You don't need to worry about it."

His mother was also annoyed. She puffed herself up, the diamond pin prominent on her chest, and said in an affected and ungainly Yiddish, "You don't have to teach him. He already had someone to teach him, thank God."

The dentist grew angry at them. "This is outrageous. My patient is waiting," he said as he headed back.

As his father heard the woman groaning, he beat his fist into his palm and said, "He should have had more practice in the hospital . . . to work with someone for a little while longer. To take such a kid . . ."

It irritated his mother that her husband should treat their son, the doctor, like some little kid. She puffed her chest with the diamond pin and said, "Now look here. Why are you trembling? Do you think these are *your* customers? He's no peddler. He has nothing to be afraid of—do you hear? Should it make the headlines? When you pull a tooth, it hurts."

But her heart was also pounding. "Who knows? It's still his first time." She bit her fingernails.

His father approached the door of the private office, got on his knees, and peered through the keyhole with one eye while making a kind of smacking sound with his lips as if to say, "Not like that, that's not right . . . twist the root, just a little, ah, ah . . ." He moved his elbows as though he were pulling a tooth.

He heard a shriek and jumped up as if on springs. His wife wrung her hands. "Oh my! Berel, come here, they're going to open that door."

Berel went and sat back down in his seat. Soon the door opened, and the woman came out with her head down. Turner came out after her, red as fire, and helped her onto the leather sofa he was paying for on installment.

The woman was shaking all over, groaning. The dentist was dismayed that the woman had yet to pay him. Who knew? Maybe she would leave and forget to pay? He looked around, ashamed to ask for what he was owed.

His father was burning to know about the money and was waiting to see when the woman would finally make to leave. At first his mother was alarmed at how the woman was shaking. But when she saw that the woman didn't faint, she felt relieved. Grateful that her son had not caused some misfortune, she went over to the woman, soothing her and starting up a long conversation.

Though still somewhat dazed, the woman was not at all sluggish and answered each question with three new ones, her voice modulated by her pain. "Your eldest son?"

"Yes, such a gift."

"Has he had the office long?"

"He's had it two years and he should have it for a hundred and twenty more."

"Do you have other children besides him?"

"Yes, each and every one a gift."

"Seems like he's just gotten his degree. How long has he been a doctor?"

His mother was terrified; this could hurt his business.

"Goodness, what are you talking about? He's been in practice for five years already. You see?" She pointed to a jar of teeth. "Pulled them himself, God's honest truth."

The woman pulled herself up to take a look. Midway she remembered the pain in her tooth and began walking feebly.

Meanwhile the father was standing with the doctor in another corner and asked him, "Tell me, has she paid?"

"Not yet."

"You're such a fool. Go over and demand it from her. Such a cheapskate, thinking she can ignore it and just walk away."

"Never mind it, Papa, she'll pay."

"How much are you thinking of charging her?"

"A dollar, I think."

"I reckon half of that. Don't push it; you're still new. That's what the one over on Delancey Street's charging."

But what they were talking about was not their biggest worry. Let it be fifty cents. The most important thing was how they were going to get her to take the hint.

Berel signaled his wife to wrap up her conversation. So she steered the woman on to a tangent, then on to three more, and then on to two further little digressions. Then all at once she stopped. The room was quiet enough to hear a fly buzzing. The silence weighed on both women's hearts; their tongues were eager, impatient, and restless. But the silence stood like an iron wall, unyielding; it lay upon them like a heap of stones. They turned gloomy. A round, smooth thing, like fish jelly, slipped off their unspeaking tongues.

The women were embarrassed to look each other in the eye because of the silence.

The father coughed, and the son began to whistle a tune, like a young man who wants to cry but feigns courage.

The father wanted to start a conversation about money, so he moaned, "Ah, such expenses, such expenses . . ."

The patient also moaned, "Such costs . . ."

"Since you'll be a little unsteady on your way home, make sure you hold on to your pocketbook; there have been pickpockets around here lately."

The woman clutched her pocketbook tightly.

The father crossed his arms behind him, looked her in the eye, and said, "Oh, the money, the money . . ."

A moment later, when the woman rose and headed for the door, the dentist let out his breath. His mother, not knowing what was happening, accompanied her, but his father took two large strides toward them and burst out, "Pardon me. You know, of course, that at a dentist's office one doesn't pester about payment. But just in case you might forget—you owe fifty cents."

The woman started as if burned. "Oh dear! I completely forgot." Then she said with some resentment, "Dear me, I'm not trying to run out on the bill. What are you so afraid of? It's the first time I've ever been pestered to pay at a dentist's office."

She angrily took out two quarters, handed them to the man, and left in a huff.

When the door closed, they huddled together and rehashed it all as a family. The father held up the money like it was a lucky charm and handed it to his son.

The young dentist turned a fiery red, buried the two quarters in his pocket, and said to his father, "Nonsense."

His mother grabbed her son and kissed him on the forehead. "My son, congratulations."

His father quietly repeated these words, stroking his beard. "Do you know what I want to tell you, my dear son? When the Lord shows you a miracle, deposit it in the bank if you want to move up in the world. It'll help the business."

The son grew talkative and cheerful, retelling the story of how it all happened. His parents drank in every word, so proud of such a son. But when it came to the part where he yanked the tooth, his father jumped up, clapping his hands. "That's my boy."

A Dance

He was standing off to the side watching the others dancing. He might have been tempted to let loose, but when you're tired after a full day's work . . . His name was Mayer. In America they called him Max, but it came out sounding like Meks. Max had only gotten married four years earlier, but his wrinkled forehead and worn-out body made his twenty-eight years look like forty.

That's how it was most days. But today, thanks to his relative's wedding, Max looked five years younger. A massage, a haircut, a shine, a new checkered suit—he had soaked it all in and felt like a million bucks.

If not for his work-weary feet, he would set the town alight. His wife stayed at home. She was feeling ill and missed the chance to see whether he could still look like a lively bachelor, athletic and confident.

The familiar music, the lightness, the guests all dressed up—*what pleasure!*

Max's heart was so full that he wanted to kiss someone. He went over to Moyshe the joiner's son, whom he hadn't seen in a long time, and offered his hand with gusto. Even though he knew they weren't related, he nevertheless congratulated him and wished him the best with all of his heart. The blessing came out effortlessly, like a pious old Jew, not the freethinker he had recently become.

Moyshe was also in the kind of high spirits that made him want to kiss everyone. He responded to Max wholeheartedly, "With God's help, it'll only be celebrations when we get to see each other."

"Amen."

"What do you do, Max?"

"What does anyone do in America? Textiles."

"Right."

"That's right."

"Still, Maxie, you seem a little upset. What's wrong? The wife pestering you?"

He winked, and Max responded with a foolish smile.

Moyshe pointed to a man in a shabby top hat. "Do you know who that is?"

"Of course I do. It's Oyzer from the old country."

"Right. Did you hear? He threw away his last dollar on real estate."

Max truly pitied him.

"That so? Poor guy. He toiled away for so many years in America—he took in eighteen boarders. He really made something of himself."

He felt a strong desire to go over and flatter him, so he would see that he was still considered a wealthy man; the sky still hadn't fallen. He went over to him.

"Hello, Oyzer! Do you recognize me?"

"Of course I do, what kind of question is that? Mayer, Brod's son. Hello! How goes it?"

Max was pleased that Oyzer recognized him. After all, here was a man who once threw around thousands as if it were nothing, invested in real estate—and now was defeated. Because Max was in such a good mood, he decided to show him respect, as if Oyzer had not lost all his money.

He looked at Oyzer with a deferential smile and waited for him to ask a question.

"How are you, Mayer? What are you doing these days?"

"What does a regular Joe do? Live off interest? He works."

The once wealthy man eyed him suspiciously, wondering whether Mayer was mocking him. His look cut Mayer to the quick: *Oyzer might think he was talking about him!* Mayer quickly tried to fix things:

"Once a beggar always a beggar."

He intended his self-effacement to stoke the wealthy man's pride. But the wealthy man didn't know he was being self-effacing, and it only served to dredge up his pain once more: *Once a beggar always a beggar.* Oyzer turned his piercing gaze on him again, and Mayer was even more cowed by that withering look, especially watching as the impoverished Oyzer cocked his head away angrily, pretending not to hear.

"Did you hear me, Oyzer?" The wealthy man turned his head with a look that said, "You lowlife. Who do you think you're talking to?"

Mayer pointed at Oyzer's diamond ring and said, "For example, that little rock is worth more than any one of us makes in a year."

The wealthy man was relieved: Mayer had meant it in earnest. He wasn't mocking him for losing all his money after all.

A lively tune started up. The parents of the bride and groom assembled and began to dance. Since Mayer was a relation, though distant, he was also dragged into the dance.

The drum and the cymbals crashed louder and louder, exciting everyone. Suddenly Mayer felt compelled to enter the circle, as quickly as possible, before something got away. A thrill ran through him, as his feet began to bounce. His youthful days flashed before his eyes, when he had longed to go to dance classes and travel to Vienna to become a clerk in a fancy haberdashery. His heart felt young once again, swelling in his chest, and beating to the rhythm of the music: *rakhta-rakhta, rakhta-ri-ram.*

The families started shouting: "Clear the way! Make room!"

With his arms akimbo, Mayer tossed his head to the left and set his feet in motion. *Rakhta-rakhta, rakhta-ri-ram.*

A circle of men gathered around. He felt it was him they were gathering around, so he tried to throw his feet out to the side as his heart sang: *rakhta-rakhta, rakhta-ri-ram.* His face blanched, and the rings around his eyes burned with fire, his sides heaving and his heart panting: *rakhta-rakhta, rakhta-ri-ram.*

He cautioned himself: "Mayer, stop. You're a father, you're going to breathe your last." To which he angrily replied, "Don't worry your head about me anymore."

People saw him drenched in sweat and gaped.

Mayer felt how intensely people were looking at him as he danced unsteadily, falling down and getting up with a *ri-ram ri-ram*, and stepping on someone's feet. Whose feet he didn't know. His heart was beating unsteadily; he was thrown to the side, knocked down and getting back up again.

The drum and the cymbals revived everyone's forgotten youth. You could see old victories, better times, and younger days on their faces. An old woman's cheeks flushed with color as she raised her skirts and began to dance. A young woman, a Yankee, stood there watching these new immigrants, her affected derision belied by the look in her eyes.

An even older man pushed his cap to the side, gave a crooked smile, and snapped his fingers, *ri-ram ri-ram.*

They yelled at Mayer: "Mayer, that's enough." . . . No, no, still . . . *ri-ram, ri-ram* . . . Dance, celebrate . . . It's a family wedding . . . We're closely related now . . . *ri-ram, ri-ram* . . . Hundred and fifty dollars, a bank book . . . *rakhta-ri-ram* . . . A candy store . . . No more having to work . . . *rakhta, rakhta-ri-ram* . . .

The music stopped suddenly, and Mayer collapsed onto a bench. The hall felt as if it was full of smoke after a fire. The smoke wasn't so much seen as felt, borne on the sweaty faces of the approaching men.

The ceremony and the dinner that followed flew by like a dream. When it was almost over, Mayer sobered up. He thought to himself that he was a close relation and should stay longer than the other guests.

As everyone began to leave, the bride took off her veil. The in-laws began talking about tomorrow's business. He realized that the wedding was finally over, causing his heart to tighten with distress. He felt a strong wave of regret for everything. Like someone who struggles to stoke a dying fire, Mayer tried to preserve the last little bit of heat in his thin bones but couldn't. He grew weary, limb by limb, and the joyous thoughts that had enlivened his dancing—or the dancing that had enlivened his thoughts— trickled away. His thoughts returned to life in a fourth-floor apartment on Suffolk Street.

There was frost outside, but even before he left he had begun shivering from the cold. He turned up the collar of his coat and pulled his fedora down over the rheumatic side of his head. People could now see he was a married man, because there were two kinds of fedora: one kind for the single man and the other for the married. The single man's hat was small and always worn rakishly on the crown of the head, leaving a young man's ear and stylish haircut exposed. The married man's hat was uniformly larger and covered half of the ear.

Mayer went to say his goodbyes first to the bride and then to her mother-in-law.

The mother-in-law struggled to keep a decorous expression on her sleepy face and mumbled in her deep drowsiness, "Why didn't you bring your missus?"

Mayer also mumbled his response because he, too, was sleepy: "Teeth are bothering her."

She mumbled again, "Could dress it with a compress."

"Tried that, but it didn't help. Now it's like two weeks after giving birth."

"Yes, so you see, *that* you've got right."

Mayer was delighted for there to be an end to all the excuses, and took his leave.

As she offered her hand, he bent in to kiss her cheek. She wasn't expecting that and failed to turn her head. When she saw that he wanted her cheek she leaned toward him, but he had already moved his head away. Yet when he saw how she did in fact want a kiss on the cheek he leaned his head toward her again, but it was already too late.

Outside a sharp wind slapped his face, and he doubled over and turned away. Strange thoughts crept into his head and ate him up inside along with the cold. For example, why, only when he was arriving at the wedding, did people embrace him lovingly, kissing on the cheeks as if it were the obvious thing to do, not turning their heads this way and that. *You fool, don't you understand? That was before dinner.*

Why had he wished Moyshe so well? Couldn't he see that he was a beggar? That's enough of that. Back home he would have been a porter, but here . . . a "steady job," making vests.

Bah, take this Oyzer from the old country. Wasn't it such a pleasure that he'd lost his shirt? He wanted to get rich quick. There's real estate for you. Slow and steady, buddy . . .

He took pleasure in the fact that Oyzer had lost his bottom dollar, all the time congratulating himself with a "well, well." But the closer he got to his home, the more troubled he became. As he ascended the dark stairs on his exhausted feet, it was torture: *What kind of candy store is he thinking of? Can you even get a candy store for a hundred and fifty dollars?* Everything that was swirling around in his mind during the dance was now starting to torment him. The musicians' *rakhta ri-ram* buzzing in his ears kept mocking him. He wanted for anything to rid himself of that little tune, but the tune did not want to rid itself of him and kept buzzing in his ears: *rakhta ri-ram, rakhta ri-ram* . . . What kind of a poor relation? To hell with it. I needed that wedding like a hole in the head. A hundred and fifty dollars?! It's the slow season. No more on the tab at the grocery, *rakhta ri-ram*, of course it's only fifty. Tomorrow I've got to pay a month's rent. I'll pay back Itiskl's eighty dollars. A beggar . . . *rakhta ri-ram*, broke again . . .

A Speech

Before anyone noticed, it was already two in the morning, but no one wanted to go home. This was the club's tenth anniversary banquet.

The members celebrated as they strode tipsily around the hall to the excessive refrains of gratuitous laughter.

One member made a motion that everyone should sing *Hatikvah*. A couple of other members cleared their throats in assent, and they began. But since everyone started on a different note and at differing tempos, they all went their own way, which in musical parlance is called a "fugue" and in plain Yiddish—everyone tripped each other up.

Kuni, Dobe's son, wandered around with a drink in his hand, repeating to himself, "Well, to your health! To your health!" And he truly meant that "to your health" with all his heart, because who was as nice a guy as Kuni? He wouldn't hurt a fly. No matter the curses someone had received, Kuni would try to make him feel better.

Kuni had but one flaw—he was a terrible public speaker. Simply put, he stuttered.

It was agony how people humiliated him. Not with words, God forbid. They couldn't do that; after all, they knew each other's families. No, everyone was respectful on the surface, but subtly, with a look, with a half-smile. He understood.

What more did he need? His own wife was no worse than a stranger. There was just that one thing—his stuttering.

Yet as if out of spite, he loved to talk. The harder it was for him to open his mouth, the more he felt impishly driven to speak. But how could he get in his side of the argument when she cut him off before the breath could even leave his mouth? They lived together just fine—what issue did he have with her? Only the one—that she never let him speak.

Wasn't it the same at the club? When he would begin saying something, Shaykele Koval would pester him with a "point of order." "Ugh, whenever we give him time!" For a while he had wanted to be a candidate for vice president. Was Shaykele really so much more important than him? The only difference was Shaykele's loud voice. When he started up with the words "I make a motion that we should not be so hasty to distribute sick benefits to a healthy member; that's my issue," everyone agreed.

And if the chairman asked if there were any objections, looking at each person individually, including Kuni, Kuni's face would turn bright red. He wanted to get up and say that yes, there was an objection; inside he was screaming, "Stand up! Speak, talk, say something!" But his feet wouldn't move.

However, when it came down to a vote, he turned into a completely different person. True, to vote you didn't have to do anything but raise a hand. But that was enough. He poured his whole soul into the effort of raising his hand. His hand would be more visible than anyone else's. He would stretch his arm stiffly, to the point of breaking, his fingers wiggling. Those fingers spoke.

Afterward a sweet pride radiated through him, and he felt like he had become more of a man.

Now, just as everyone was ready to have a good time, some joker whispered to the toastmaster that he should give the floor to Kuni. Kuni was sitting off to the side, watching and listening to everything. This was all a novelty to him, the first time he had ever been to a banquet. He had been in America for eight years and already had grandchildren, thank God, but he had never seen such a thing. This was neither a ball nor a wedding, but it was still a joyous occasion. Add to that the speeches.

How jealous he was of the president and the vice president that they were giving speeches.

When all of a sudden he heard his name called out, he felt a little tickle in his heart; he didn't know what was happening to him.

Someone stood him on a chair and told him to speak.

Everything went dark, then all at once became bright as sparks flew. He started to tremble on the chair. Two members came over and held him up by the sides, laughing. Meanwhile, people started shouting, "Come on! Order please!" The thought suddenly occurred to him: "It's for your sake people are screaming 'order please.'"

The hall fell so silent you could hear a fly buzzing. Kuni looked like a corpse; he had no idea what was happening to him. The one thing he did feel was people staring at him. *Perhaps he had fainted and they were trying to revive him?*

But when he heard the toastmaster's voice—"Kuni Ziselman, go ahead and speak. Order, please!"—he stirred weakly, his lips started moving as if in a dream, and in an alien voice repeated, "Order, please."

Slowly he recovered. First an ear turned red, then a cheek, then both ears and both cheeks. He became aware of himself standing on a chair in a hall with people standing around watching him and waiting for him to speak. The time was now—no one was interrupting him. On the contrary, he could speak as much as they would listen. This wasn't home, and he wasn't at work, standing at the iron.

So he started talking. From the very first he spoke with difficulty, stuttering, speeding up out of habit—in case they didn't let him keep talking—getting jumbled up. But he spoke, and spoke, and spoke.

He spoke about this world and the next, about home, about the shop, about politics. His tongue got twisted, as if smeared with butter. At times he stuttered, and sometimes he just stopped. But he kept talking. He spoke about all the things that in the thirty-five years since his wedding he had never mentioned. He described how ultimately evil people would be punished and receive their just reward; and that the Eternal One was patient and repaid well. Apparently he was referring to those who humiliated him.

At the beginning, just as he had started to speak, he heard a smattering of suppressed laughter and some teasing. But gradually, the more he spoke the more serious the audience became, and they really started to listen.

Shaykele Koval tried to crack jokes off to the side: "Look, he's learned to speak!"

When Kuni got down from the chair, he exhaled like steam from a teapot pouring out boiling water. The fact that people were applauding befuddled him. Still something was missing. What if his wife were here.

Then he started feeling the pull of home, even though it was going quite well in the hall. Shaykele himself had come up to him and said, "You gave a great speech! You really gave it to 'em." *Can you picture this Shaykele? A nobody, just lucky. That's how it is in America. And still he's got diamonds, a cottage in Brownsville.*

The whole way home his heart was pounding. Even if he had discovered a treasure, he still wouldn't have been as happy. He felt as though he had struck it rich. *Speech, such a valuable thing. Everything was going to be different now. She was finally going to let him speak. That's saying something! Members of a club had taken their seats and had asked him to give a speech, with respect.*

It was early morning when he got home. His wife, Nekhe, was already awake and puttering around the kitchen. As he crossed the threshold and glanced at her sober, poorly rested face, he felt a little crestfallen. But his heart beat with pride. How to begin?

"Nekhe. Are you listening?"

Nekhe looked to the side. He already knew that this was a bad sign: soon she would erupt. It was always like this when he went somewhere on his own. Jealous that he hadn't taken her with him.

His voice weakened, "Nekhe."

She interrupted him, "What's new? Night after night off gallivanting around. While I suffer."

"Nekhe, don't be silly. Listen."

"I already know. I've heard it all before. Doesn't it occur to you that your poor wife might need something too?"

"Shush, quiet, just hear me out first. Two words, just listen."

But he suddenly felt as if his power of speech had disappeared. His tongue tangled up, his brain froze, and he stood there like an oaf. The thought suddenly occurred to him that it was all in vain. She would never believe him. Even if he brought the whole club in as witnesses. She knew him otherwise.

He felt like a failure. He saw that here in his house, in his kitchen, lay the truth. Out there was just a dream.

When Nekhe finally asked, in an angry tone, what the big news was that he was so fired up about, he waved his hand dismissively and said, "Ah, it's nothing. Someone gave a speech."

Sisters

The winter had passed, and it had grown rather cozier in the house. The bright days started shining into its three rooms, where the two sisters knitted neckties.

They were twins, even though Gosi looked around fifty and Poli looked thirty.

Frail Gosi had a chronic cough and always went around swathed in a dark wool blouse.

Poli on the other hand loved bright colors. Her green or sky-blue clothes against her dyed blonde hair dazzled the eyes.

Where the one wore only black velvet shoes on account of her rheumatism, the other wore the *leytist* fashion—gray, champagne, or red, but always with high heels.

Both women were short and thin, and everyone said they'd been knitting for likely twenty years.

Gosi had money in the bank as well as diamonds, sable trimmings already ten years out of date, and a fur coat also out of date. That's what she used to wear to deliver their knitting. Each new season saw her make a new *stayelish* suit and hang it in a wardrobe. There it hung till another suit was hung over it. A considerable number of suits accumulated in this way, all in the *leytist* styles. A new season, a new suit in the wardrobe.

They never went anywhere. They remained closeted in their three rooms. They jointly subscribed to a Yiddish newspaper and would read it aloud together. Mostly they talked about *next door*, about Mr. Friedman the widower and his youngest daughter, "the maiden."

Gosi loved being right. Her life's pleasure consisted in always being right. So she studied how to argue straight to the point, and everyone had to give in. It seemed she wanted nothing more than for people to let her be right. Even when someone admitted she was right, she wouldn't let it go. She took hold of the issue, and tackling every angle, she demonstrated how *right* she was.

But when all was said and done, she was still not happy. It seemed to her she could still be more right.

One morning, when the sun was already burning in the sky, Gosi called to Poli, "I think I'll go get some material for a suit."

Poli gave a *dat's rayt*, she should go.

"I don't know what's in. I think panne velvet."

Since it happened to be a weekend, she went from store to store all day long picking up samples of velvet to bring home. When she got home, she started giving her opinion:

"Can you imagine, Poli, the *kvality* material costs three dollars a yard, and this one costs four."

Poli, whose English wasn't as good as Gosi's, still answered in English, "*Vell, I don' know.*"

"I think four dollars a yard is too much. After all, I don't wear a suit for more than a season. What do you think, Poli? Is it worth it to invest so much money? Velvet's a heavy material. We're heading into summer. I think three dollars a yard is enough. More than enough."

Gosi wanted to be even more right still and kept arguing, "And those stores—everything looks so *fensy*. But in two months it'll all be out of style."

Poli nodded. "Sure."

"On the other hand, someone's going to buy it anyway. It costs three now and it'll go up to four. I hate making a fool of myself, so tomorrow I'll just buy it and make the suit. And you know, a suit like that, when it's really such good *kvality*, one can make it work for two seasons. You can say what you like—I'm only for what's good. Common is common."

"Sure, you're right."

"Am I right? Trimming costs money, tailoring costs money. Why shouldn't it be from a good material? For the sake of a dollar should I spoil a whole suit?"

Poli had nothing to add and instead told her how yesterday she'd had an argument with the floor manager of the department store.

Gosi listened and was proud she had a sister who only shopped at "department stores" and had "arguments" with "floor managers."

People said Poli had been beautiful before she turned into an old maid. She'd lived it up, made dates, gone out with boys, got disappointed, made other dates, only to be disappointed once more.

Gosi, on the other hand, was always a silent type, taciturn, stubborn. And while nobody blamed her, she didn't want to go to parties, always staying quietly at home, obstinately waiting for something.

They used to hate each other in those days, fighting like cats and dogs and calling each other nasty names. But the older they got, the less they argued. Poli grew more restrained, not as much of the "set the world on fire" type, while Gosi became talkative.

Particularly in the last couple of years, when Mr. Friedman the widower moved in next door, they had become like two good friends.

Mr. Friedman was a miser who would lend two spare dollars with interest and always worked overtime. He worked as a cloak presser and had his youngest daughter living with him, a girl of eighteen. People said he hadn't gotten married again because it cost too much money. He was too stingy to pay for another woman's meals.

That was the Mr. Friedman the two of them would talk about. They hated that girl of his to death. She should be so lucky to be a stepdaughter to someone like him.

When the new suit was ready, Gosi did several turns in front of the mirror, saying, "It fits nice." Then another look in the mirror before taking it off and hanging it in the wardrobe.

"When the 'maiden' sees this, she'll burst."

"Let her burst. Who cares?"

"Listen, I went out today, and he's standing there, Mr. Friedman, and says good morning, and opens the door for me."

"What were you wearing?"

"The sky-blue vest with the white piping."

"Lovely."

"I'm telling you, the way he pitched himself forward and said good morning. The way he opened the door for me."

"Never mind. You think he only does that for you? Yesterday I'm standing on the stoop, and he comes over to me and grasps my hand. I tell you, I was surprised. So he grasps me by the hand." They both giggled.

That same evening they were sitting and chatting. Gosi held forth: "I'm telling you, it's not worth the effort. Take Mr. Friedman as an example. What wife could do well with him? Stingy, denying life's pleasures. Going around dressed like a beggar. What pipe dreams he's cooking up. If he loans fifty dollars on interest, what, he makes a hundred. I hate to make a fool of myself; after all he's not a young man. There's also the 'maiden.' Who knows how much a 'maiden' like that can owe her father."

"Sure, you're right."

"And when you get right down to it, what good would come from that?"

"Sure."

"On the other hand, it's not the worst thing. A man makes a living. The little children he's got . . . Ugh! If only that 'maiden' would go off with some young man. Otherwise she'll stay a dutiful daughter, and he'll never need a wife. But at the same time, he's still a man who lends money on interest. Right?"

"Yes."

"So what, a young *boychik* is better? Playing cards and wasting his time *dencing*. At least a stable man . . . So what if he's a little stingy. *Vell*, a person's got to have some kind of defect. So then, let me tell you, if you want to save a penny you've got to be stingy, otherwise you'll come to nothing. Am I right or not? No, I just want to know if I'm right or not!"

"Sure. You're right."

THE FINAL STORY

A Fur Salesman

Volky, a tall, stout man with a houseful of children, argues with his wife. A slap from time to time. But he likes his job. Not the work so much as the haggling. He sells furs to the local gentiles. There are quite a few here in Canada. He takes out a fur cap and twirls it around in his hands for a gentile customer: "You see what this is, goy?"

How much does he want for it?

He takes a big step backward, away from the gentile, and trains his eyes on him. Piercing him. Consuming him with a smile.

How much does he want for it?

He twists his head to one side and then the other like a chicken on a coop ladder. He starts drawing the gentile in. He claps his hands.

"Five dollars!"

Slowly he starts moving away, coyly.

In the gentile's hesitation he knows he won't pay that much.

"How much'll you give me for it, goy?"

The gentile still doesn't pay.

Again the merchant backs away, smiling, squinting an eye, but all the while looking the gentile flirtingly in the face. His silence saps the gentile, who starts shifting from one foot to the other. Then he claps his hand.

"Four and a half!"

He approaches once more till the gentile is drawn in. On the next Sabbath he meets up with his compatriots and boasts, "That goy comes running over the next day with his cap. 'Volky, it's shedding! And I haven't got another four dollars. Here, just look, it's shedding. Is it shedding or isn't it?' Goyim are all boors. When he bought it, he didn't test the fur, but now he does. So the goy, he's crying, imagine it, just crying away. And I don't know if he's drunk or not. But I see his eyes are wet—I should only see a nice round thousand this year as easily—and don't you know but I've still got those four dollars in my pocket. I've got the four dollars, and he's got the shedding cap. My heart goes out to him, and I give him back the money."

"So, what was wrong with it? Was it moths? Had moths gotten to it?"

"What else? You think I'd have given him a quality fur for four dollars? I'm quite partial to a fine fur."

"Where on earth do you put the nice furs?"

"It's a sin to get rid of nice furs! They can just sit there. It's cash; it's money in the bank. They can just sit and sit."

Volky's no liar. He'd sell his wife and children for a quality fur. A nice fur he'd put right in bed with him so when he wakes up in the middle of the night he can pet it. A nice fur he can look at with pride on the Sabbath.

But when he's buying, he's a completely different person. Here's how it goes:

Charles, the little Frenchman, stands in his peasant coat covered in frost. He's standing there with the furs over his shoulder, next to Volky. Volky is angry. His son, the little pest, is getting underfoot with the wagon he had made himself. His father lifts his boots swiftly, turns red as a beet, and stamps on the wagon. "Take that!"

The wagon lies there trampled to bits as the little boy cries.

"Take that!"

His mother saves what pieces she can, holding back her tears, and gets a boot to her hand. The wound turns red, bleeds, but she doesn't even rub it. *Let it bleed so he can see, the murderer.* But the murderer roars:

"Bastards, damn you! Go away, filthy woman! And take him with you, or you can just kick off. Leave me alone! Let me earn a living! Nothing but nuisances. To hell with you!"

In front of a customer Volky can suppress his anger. But now he's buying, so there's no harm.

Charles, the little Frenchman, is standing there with the furs over his shoulder, motionless. He is frozen in place. Expressionless. He's used to the act. Volky spins toward him.

"What do you want?"

The silver fox over his shoulder has caught his eye for some time.

The Frenchman turns toward the door without a word. Volky realizes his act has gone a bit too far but still he pretends he hasn't seen the silver fox. He sniffs.

"What've you got there, muskrats?"

Charles takes three lynx furs out of his bag.

"Lynxes."

Volky tosses the lynxes onto the table.

"What are these, dead cats?"

His enemies say Volky occasionally skins dead cats. He gives each one a whack.

"This is good, fresh lynx!"

ezes, lost in thought. Maybe about the lynx den. A family
one, only cleaner. The mother lies inside, suckling and
, and bringing her little ones what she can. A mother
voice with her children. She teaches them manners;
cleans her boys' silky fur; she takes them in her paws,
and gives them a kick. She teaches them how to play,
ht an enemy, to scratch at its eyes, or to spit at it, and
aches them how to wash, how to smooth their whis-
their claws on the bark of a tree, how to fold an ear
, how to go outside to warm themselves in the sun and
their ears.
t for the dead cats?"
it's fresh lynx."
the two sons and the daughter have grown, and their
nd their eyes sparkle and shine at night, then they'll
ll bicker and fight with one another; they'll grab at
whiskers; they'll bite each other for fun, then turn
ot with their silky flame-red tongues so they won't
harm. Their mother shows them tricks, capering on
ny. She pricks up her ears, flashes her eyes, and leaps
es out and starts creeping on her belly, very slow-
that squirrel at the top of the tree? It's eating nuts! You
ack, to pounce, to draw the soul out of a living thing,
ou eat, and while you're eating, to pounce again and
d there a caress . . .
ys and weeks he sits in the trembling oak and waits.
has left her den, sneaks up and shoots them all right
vs shoots right in the eye.
er fox.

ed out the fox and tossed it on the table. He sweeps
, two in front and one below, among the other furs
table.
rags the third fur back out. Two boys and a girl.
,"
oo, down onto the ground and turns aside.
;, brushes off all the furs and puts them back over
turned gloomy. Charles cannot go anywhere else.
o the city too often. They're looking for him in

connection to an old crime. Charles occasionally sneaks into an unfamiliar area. But Volky doesn't know the situation. He's stuck here among the Jews knowing hardly any English and no French at all. If Volky knew.

Volky becomes more important to him precisely because he doesn't know.

"What'll you give me for the lynxes?"

"I won't take the cats. Enough carcasses."

"You want the silver fox?"

"A silver? Where've you got a silver? These little white bits? Nothing to see. Bring me a real silver fox and I'll pay a good price. I pay the best."

"What'll you give me for this?"

"Nothing! I don't want it! It's not real!"

Volky foams at the mouth and turns beet red.

"That's your merchandise? A silver fox?"

He yanks it off Charles's shoulder and throws it down again on the table.

Charles has already forgotten the hard months of wandering and pursuit and the two frostbitten fingers. Others trappers have stories to tell, the kind you find in books. One of them fell into a cave where a hibernating bear was suckling her cub. She cuddled and suckled him, too, licking him like he were her own. Since she was asleep, she didn't notice. Another fell through an ice-hole on the river and got stuck, then the movies came and took a picture and rescued him in the nick of time. Another lay feverish in a tent as wild dogs brought him food to eat. People sit by the fire and tell stories.

Nothing like that had happened to Charles, just two frostbitten fingers and long months of wandering and quietly waiting, not moving, frozen still for hours on end just like up in the oak. The fox is over here and now it's over there. A sudden sighting on a snowy peak two or three miles away; it appears, turns its pointy, clever snout toward him, and smiles. Fox kits know how to smile. Charles is no liar, wouldn't make up adventures. With him there are only the long hours of waiting in the cold and the two frostbitten fingers.

Volky opens with a fiver. Yells, stamps, carries on. Again yells, stamps, carries on.

When he hears Charles relent to ten dollars, he starts laughing and mocking him. His laughter is meant to hide the greed that has begun to glint in his eyes. Charles has to throw in the three lynxes.

That night the silver fox is lying by itself on the table. Spread out. An only child. Volky's not tossing it around anymore. He's petting it as if asking its forgiveness. He turns his head toward it, first one way then another, and on his face is the smile one gives to one's bride after the wedding.

But for a hundred such Charleses! And not so much the Charleses as their shoulders. The shoulder's the important bit. A shoulder carrying a silver fox. Oh, if only the foxes would come trotting over on their own, cast off their pelts, and run away in their bare bones. But that's why one needs shoulders.

"You, come over here," he says to his wife.

The little bags under her tearful eyes obediently look up.

"What do you say to that, eh? Is your husband a salesman or what?"

Her downcast eyes stare submissively.

"Ten dollars. A real fortune! Just give it a feel. Diamonds, jewels, silver and gold! So is your husband a salesman or what?"

He takes a look around to see if the little ones are watching, then takes her by the chin: "Is your husband a salesman?!"